A PSYCHOLOGICAL THRILLER

THE MONSTER

JOCELYN SMITH

Monsters don't always lurk
under your bed

The Monster

Jocelyn Smith

Published by Jocelyn Smith, 2023.

THE MONSTER

First edition. May 25, 2023.

Copyright © 2023 Jocelyn Smith.

ISBN: 979-8223620136

Written by Jocelyn Smith.

Table of Contents

Chapter 1

JAKE MORRIS WAS FROM an all-American family or that's how they looked to the outside world. He was the youngest in the family. His mother and father had been married for years and seemed to have a loving relationship. They were the epitome of everyone who knew them. He and his brother played sports at the local high school. He was a linebacker in football. He was a good-looking young man with his arctic blue eyes and short, dark brown hair. His face was sculpted, his body muscular and he had a zest for life. He was of average size and build.

His older brother Tate, who is two years older, was better-looking than him. He had piercing baby blue, Paul Newman eyes, light brown short hair, a chiseled chin, and was on the slender side. He played basketball. He was a forward. He was also very timid. He didn't talk much but had friends he hung with. He was awkward around girls, he didn't date much even though the girls drooled over him.

Their father, Ray, was a veteran of Vietnam. He went to the Marine Corps shortly after graduating high school in 1972. He had received a purple heart for getting wounded in battle. It also ended his career in the military. He met Carly when he came home from the hospital. Carly was a beautiful young woman with curly blonde hair. She had a smile that would make anyone feel at ease. She worked as a waitress at the local grill.

Ray was dressed in his blue jeans and button-up shirt. He had grabbed his duffle bag from underneath the Greyhound bus and walked into the grill. He looked around the small restaurant before finding a seat at one of the booths. He put his duffle bag on one side of the booth and sat on the other. He wasn't sitting at the booth long before Carly showed up. She was chipper when she greeted him.

CARLY WAS WEARING HER pink uniform and soft sole non-slip shoes during her shifts at the grill. After work, she would walk home and get ready to attend her night classes. She was going to college to become a nurse. When Ray saw her at the grill on his first day home, it was love at first sight for him. She smiled as she waited on him at his table. She spoke in a soft southern drawl and those beautiful blue eyes of hers just drew him in. He stuttered slightly as he gave her his order for eggs over-easy, bacon, and toast with a cup of coffee. She smiled at him as his face flushed. She poured him a cup of coffee and took his order to the kitchen. He watched as she walked away.

Carly shortly returned to his booth and handed him his food. She sat it gently on the table in front of him and asked him if he needed anything else. He smiled at her and told her no and thanked her. Ray sat in the booth eating his breakfast and watching Carly as she worked. She would glance over at him periodically and see him looking back at her. She would just smile at him and he'd start eating from his plate.

When Ray was finished with his meal Carly came over to his table and left his ticket for him to pay. She smiles at him as she walks away. He leaves a ten-dollar tip, grabs his duffle bag, and walks to the register to pay. Carly rings up his ticket. He smiles at her while getting money out of his wallet to hand to her. She asks him if he enjoyed the meal and he tells her he did. He smiles at her as he speaks. She hands him his change and his receipt, leaving her number on the back. He walks outside and walks toward his parent's home.

He walks the two-mile trek with his green duffle bag strap over his shoulder. When he gets to the end of the drive where his family's farm is he opens the mailbox, grabs the mail inside, and walks the quarter-mile up the drive. His mother, Elsie was on the porch watering her big ferns when she saw someone walking up the driveway. She puts her hand on her forehead and over her eyes to try to make out who it was. She starts running toward Ray when she realizes it was her son.

Ray's father, Frank, had been in the barn when he arrived. Elsie gives Ray a hug and kiss on the cheek and welcomes him home. Ray hands her the mail he grabbed from the mailbox. She was glad her son was home. Last she and Frank had heard were that Ray had been shot and was in the hospital getting treatment. They didn't know that he was coming home.

Frank emerged from the side of the farmhouse after he heard a commotion. Elsie was overjoyed when she saw Ray and screamed out. Frank had heard and got worried. He had his pitchfork in his hands in case he was going to have to come to her defense. Frank had been in the barn raking hay for their horses. When he sees Ray, he drops the pitchfork, walks over, hugs him, and welcomes him home. He was elated that his son was home safe.

Elsie makes her homemade meatloaf dinner that Ray loves and they all sit at the dining room table, eating and talking. Ray tells them about some of his time overseas in Vietnam. His mother gasps at the horror of it all. Ray doesn't tell them everything but just the jest of it and even that is horror-filled enough. A couple of his friends went home in caskets. They were members of his battalion. After that night, Ray never spoke of his time in Vietnam again. He just pushed it back into the depths of his memory and moved forward with his life.

He heads upstairs to his room. While he's unpacking, he gets the receipt from the diner out of his back jeans pocket. He looked and saw the number Carly had given to him. He thinks about calling her but instead sticks it in the crevasse of his dresser mirror. He rushes out the door. He goes to the barn and saddles up his old mare and takes off down the road. He wants to go exploring and see the beautiful sunset fall along the hill at the end of the property.

When he returns, he puts his mare up and heads inside. He showers and lays in bed. He eventually falls asleep. He dreams of being back in Vietnam. He wakes up in a cold sweat, panting. It is now storming outside. He can see flashes of lightning come in through his bedroom window. The thunder crackles and shakes the house afterward. He rolls over on his stomach, puts the pillow over his head, and falls back asleep. He wakes up the next morning, gets dressed, and comes downstairs to eat breakfast. He will be working in the fields until dusk.

Ray and Frank work in the fields baling hay all week. Ray is getting a farmer's tan from the fieldwork. He called Carly earlier in the day and made plans for dinner and a movie for the night. When the sun is getting lower in the afternoon sky, Frank and Ray call it a day and head in. Ray gets showered and ready for his date with Carly. He kisses his mother on the cheek and tells his father bye as he heads out to his 1972 Chevelle and gets in and drives off.

He picks Carly up from the diner before heading to the movies. They're going to the local drive-in movie theatre which is showing a double feature. The first movie is Herbie Rides Again. Carly and Ray both laugh during the movie. During the interval and before Texas Chainsaw Massacre begins they go to the concession stand and order burgers, fries, and drinks. They go sit back in the Chevelle and wait for the second movie to start.

Carly isn't a fan of horror movies. While watching the Texas Chainsaw Massacre she digs her head into Ray's chest to cover her eyes from the bloody massacre on the big screen. Ray kind of chuckles at her because she's hiding her face. He's seen worse horror than the chainsaw-wielding Leatherface. He consoles her, putting his arm around her to shield her from the violence.

She has her arm around him and while her head is buried in his chest, she smells his cologne. It's the old spice smell she's used to from working at the grill. A lot of men wear it. She likes the smell of it. She eventually looks up at him and sees that he's staring down at her. She takes his cheeks in her small hands and kisses him passionately. She quickly backs away and apologizes. He tells her it's fine and then he moves over and kisses her.

That night, at the drive-in they make out. After they leave, Ray drives her home. He walks her to her door and kisses her before he leaves. She asks him if he would like to come in and have some coffee. He declines, telling her he has an early morning and long day tomorrow. She goes inside, he leaves in his Chevelle toward home.

The next day he works in the fields loading hay boxes on the back of his father's flat-bed diesel truck. He and Carly made plans again for tonight. When it's starting to get dark out, they head inside. Ray gets ready for his second date with Carly. They're going for a walk along the beach at the lake. The lake is only twenty minutes away. When Carly gets in the Chevelle, she sits next to Ray. They drive out to the lake and get out of the car. They head down the walking path toward the lake's edge.

There's nobody at the beach. Many are out in their boat fishing. Carly lays a blanket down on the beach. They're going to watch the stars overhead. There is supposed to be a meteor shower and they don't want to miss it. Ray sits beside Carly on the blanket and puts his arm around her. They look up to the night sky and see their first falling stars. Carly makes a wish as one falls. Ray just looks on. He remembers laying in the fields of Vietnam at night, wide awake looking up at the stars past the treetops wishing to make it home.

They fall back on the blanket with Carly's head in the bend of Ray's arm. They watch as it seems a million stars fall from the sky above. They talk about future plans and life. They make out under the stars, kissing each other passionately. Carly and Ray both stop before going too far as Carly is religious and believes in waiting until marriage.

Each day the two of them spend together. Eventually, Ray proposes to Carly using his grandmother's old engagement ring. It was a small diamond with a blue sapphire ring. Carly loved it. He proposed to her during her shift at the diner. He walks in and stops her at the door. The patrons looked on as he got on bended knee and asked her. She said yes and they kissed. The patrons clapped and congratulated both.

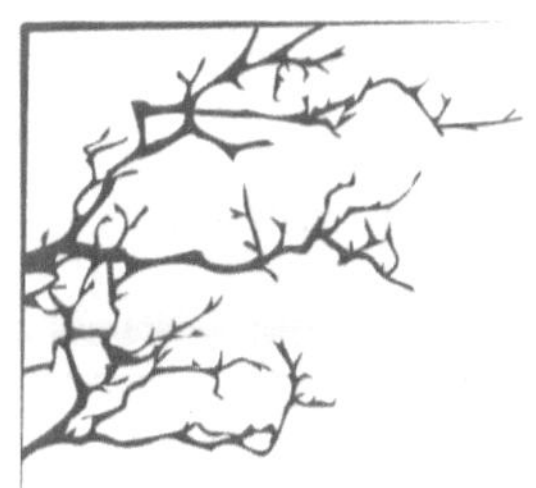

Chapter 2

It's June 1975. The Vietnam war has ended. Ray is at the baptist church standing and waiting. Carly is putting on her mother's wedding dress and veil. She grabs her red and white bouquet of roses. She walks out of the dressing room toward her father, John, who was standing in the entryway of the church waiting. She put her arm through his and the double doors of the church opened. Carly and her father walked down the aisle toward the bridegroom. Ray was dressed in his black suit. He had a red rose pinned to his right chest. They both smiled as they greeted each other at the podium. Their Sunday preacher was doing their vows.

After the ceremony had ended, the bride and groom went to their new home. It was Carly's house, Ray had moved his belongings in. Now it was their house. Carly's parents had bought it for her as a graduation present. She had finished nursing school and was now working at the local county general hospital. Ray had gotten a job driving a bus for the city and worked at the local food mart bagging groceries and loading them into customers' cars.

That night Carly and Ray had intercourse. Ray wasn't a virgin and had sex during his time in the Marines with women of different backgrounds. Carly was a virgin. Ray had to take it easy with her. She was nervous. They have sex several more times during the night.

Carly ends up pregnant within a month. Nine months later, she goes into labor while at work. She gives birth to Tate. Tate is a happy, beautiful baby boy with his mother's baby blue eyes. Carly has an easy birth with him, laboring for only five hours. Ray helps her out with Tate when he isn't working or sleeping. Carly took a few weeks off from her nursing job to tend to the baby after his birth.

Life in the Morris household was going well. Ray was making a lot of money at his jobs. They bought a second car. Their home was a three-bedroom house in a nice, quiet neighborhood. Carly had friends in the neighborhood and from work that would come and visit. Ray would have cookouts on Friday nights and play football with his friends at the park nearby. During the late summer months, he would help his father in the fields. He would come home exhausted.

Two years have passed. Carly is pregnant again. She is still working as a nurse at the local hospital. This pregnancy has been more difficult for her. Her ankles are swollen. Her doctor tells her she's at risk for pre-eclampsia. Her doctor instructs her that she needs to stay off her feet and rest more. Carly only has two months to go before her due date is up. She takes time off from work and does as the doctor instructs, or tries to. It's hard when you have a two-year-old running amok through the house. Carly calls her mother, Judy, and asks her to help.

Six weeks have passed and Carly is in the hospital. Her blood pressure is at dangerous levels. She has to have the baby or is at risk of dying. They perform an emergency C-section to deliver Jake. Ray is there when she wakes up in recovery. Jake looks more like his father. Elsie dotes over Jake. She wants to help Carly take care of him until she is recovered. Carly has no issues with it.

Carly is in a lot of pain and is taking prescription pain killers. She sleeps most of the time. Elsie takes care of Jake and Tate while Ray is working. Judy even comes over to help out with the boys. It takes almost six weeks for Carly to recover from the emergency surgery. She has spent minimal time with both of her boys during her recovery. She appreciates the help from Elsie and Judy but now that she's feeling better, she would prefer to take over on her own.

Five years go by. Frank dies. Ray, Carly, and the boys move to the farm to help Elsie out. Elsie pampers Jake more than she does Tate. She gives Jake anything he wants when others aren't around. Carly is still working at the hospital and Ray has now taken on the farm, quitting his jobs with the supermarket and the city bus. He spends most of his time working the farm. He makes Tate and Jake help him feed the animals. Tate loves feeding them. Jake is a little more resistant to the work.

A few more years go by and Ray takes the boys out in the field to teach them how to shoot a rifle. He wants to go on a hunting trip this fall with them to teach them about hunting. Jake is happy to learn. Tate is also. Frank had taken Ray on many hunting trips growing up. They hunt on the first day of the season. Ray shoots and kills a big buck while both boys look on in amazement. He puts the buck on his shoulders and they all walk back home. Ray hangs the deer from his rear feet in one of the smaller buildings designated as the hunting barn. His father and he gutted many deer, turkey, and elk in this barn over the years.

Jake is amused watching his father cut the deer from end to end. Ray sticks his hands inside, pulling out all of the deer's internal organs and dropping them in a five-gallon bucket below. Tate gets a little nauseous and asks if he can leave. Ray tells him he can and Tate runs off into the house. Elsie cracks a few jokes about Tate and his weakness. She tells him to grow a pair of balls, that's how farm life is. Carly hears and talks to Elsie about it. Tate is a sensitive child. He doesn't like violence. Neither does Carly.

The next season, the three are out hunting again. This time Jake wants to take the buck down. Ray lets him shoot. Jake's aim is superb. He hits the buck in his shoulder and it falls to the ground. Ray has to carry the buck home as it's too heavy for Jake. Tate watches this time as Jake guts the deer with his father's instructions. Jake is enjoying it, smiling as he cuts the deer open.

It's now 1992, Tate and Jake are now in junior high. Jake is a freshman while Tate is a junior. Jake loves getting attention from his classmates. Many would say he's the class clown. Some of the girls don't like him. They think he's crazy. Jake likes talking about hunting to his friends at school. He tells them about gutting and skinning deer, about how cool it is to cut off the meat, and how easy it is for him to do.

Tate keeps to himself mostly at school. He is well-liked and many of the students know he's smart. He even tutors some of them at times, staying after school to help them get passing grades. At times students come over to his house. They used the dining room table to study. Jake likes interrupting them a lot.

Carly works mostly during the day now. She's home before the boys get home from school. Ray is home all the time working in the fields. Tate helps him with gathering hay during the summer months. Jake makes a big deal just to get out of helping. Elsie gives Jake ice cream after he comes in from the fields. Tate just goes upstairs to shower.

It's fall again, which means deer season in the Morris household. Jake is ecstatic to go. Tate asks if he can stay home this time. His father lets him stay. After Ray and Jake return home from hunting, Tate and Jake are sitting in the living room. Jake is cleaning his rifle. Tate is watching television, not paying attention to Jake. Carly, Ray, and Elsie are in the dining room talking. All of a sudden and loud pop sound is heard. Carly and Ray run into the living room and see Tate lying on the floor with blood pouring out of his chest. They both run over to him. Elsie is on the phone calling an ambulance.

Carly grabbed a towel from the pile of laundry on the sofa, pressing it down over the wound. She is holding Tate's hand, crying and pleading with him to stay with them. Ray is crying, stroking Tate's head as Tate takes his final gargled, breath. Jake is just standing there looking on. Elsie is also, with her hands on Jake's shoulders. Ray stands up and walks quickly to Jake asking him what happened. Jake just stands there and doesn't answer. Ray takes the rifle from his hands and sits it down on the floor. Carly is screaming and crying. She looks over at the other three, tears running down her face, eyes red from crying. She keeps asking why.

The ambulance arrives ten minutes later. Tate is pronounced dead. The sheriff's office is also there. They have to investigate to see what happened. Jake is in awe at everything that has happened. He stays silent. He just watches as they load Tate's dead body unto the gurney, cover him with a sheet and exit the room. The sheriff's office has already taken photos of the body. Carly is still sitting on the floor where her son's body was. She's covered in his blood. She's sobbing uncontrollably. She can't speak, she's too upset.

Elsie talks to the Sheriff outside. She tells him that she doesn't know what happened. She explains that she, Carly, and Ray were all in the dining room when they heard this loud pop sound. When they went to look, Jake was standing holding his rifle toward the floor and Tate was lying on the floor bleeding. Ray told the sheriff the same story. Jake wasn't talking to anyone. He was just watching everything that was happening.

The sheriff takes Jake to the sheriff's office. Elsie follows. She will sit in with them while he's being questioned. Ray stays home to try and console Carly. The sheriff takes Jake to an interrogation room. Jake just sits there and doesn't speak. He doesn't answer any of the questions. The sheriff is starting to suspect that the boy is in shock and that the shooting was accidental.

Two days go by. Tate is laying in his blue coffin. His face was a pale powdery color from the makeup not like his normal flawless-looking, chiseled face. His skin was cold and leathery to the touch. He looks like he's sleeping. He's wearing his Sunday clothes. Carly is still too upset to speak to mourners. Ray, Elsie, and Jake all meet and thank the mourners for showing up. Tate's schoolmates all attend. The girls are crying as are most of the boys. The preacher speaks about Tate and his accomplishments in his short life. Ray is holding Carly in his arms while they sit in the front row. Elsie is hugging Jake. Carly's parents are also there crying and upset that their grandson is gone. Tate's basketball teammates carry his coffin from the hearse to the grave. Tate was buried next to his grandfather, Frank at the church cemetery.

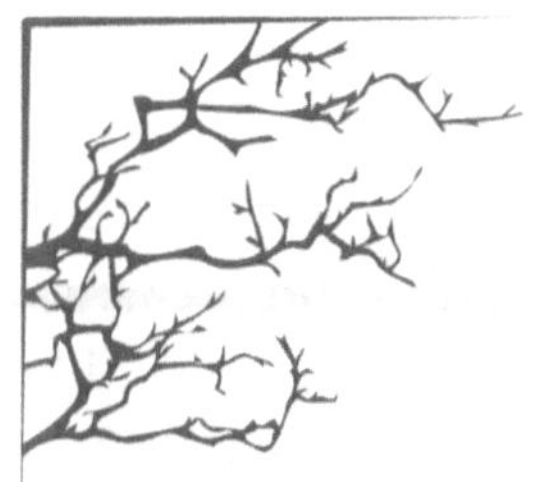

Chapter 3

After Tate's death, Carly spends most of her time working. She doesn't want to be at the house. Elsie takes care of Jake after school. Ray spends his time working the farm. Carly has nightmares every night when she falls asleep. Even when she takes a small nap at work the nightmares of that night come back. Eventually, she starts staying at her house in the city. She doesn't want to go back to the farmhouse and look in the living room and see her son lying dead on the floor. It haunts her. She withdraws from the family.

Ray visits her often, he misses her at home. They argue a lot over what happened. Jake stays with his father and grandmother. Carly spends all of her time working. She takes double shifts at the hospital. She eventually collapses while on duty one night from exhaustion. She is admitted. Everyone she works with knows what she has been dealing with. They treat her with fluids until she is better. She is released the next day. The hospital makes her take time off.

Jake enters his sophomore year. Many of the girls feel bad for him because he lost his brother. He cracks jokes with his friends at lunch. One day he talks about his brother and what happened, making jokes about it. A couple of the girls overhear it. They keep it to themselves. One of Jake's friends is having a party Friday night. Jake attends. During the party, he's dancing with several of the girls from school. They're all drinking and having a wonderful time.

Jake and Camille are dancing drunkenly to a slow song playing. They kiss and walk to one of the bedrooms. They are making out. When Camille tells Jake to stop, Jake grabs her hands and holds her down. He puts a pillow over her face to muffle her sounds as he rapes her. She passes out during the rape. Jake leaves the room after covering her up with a blanket and putting her head on a pillow.

Over the course of his sophomore year, Jake rapes a total of ten girls at his friend's parties. None of them come forward to press charges. They all blame themselves for getting drunk and becoming vulnerable.

During their 1993 graduation, Tate is remembered by his fellow classmates. The yearbook even has a remembrance page of him. Jake and his family are asked to come to the graduation for a ceremony to honor Tate. Carly comes. She stands next to Jake and Ray as the commentator speaks about Tate. The school made a scholarship fund in remembrance of Tate. They also had a marble memorial built for him that will stand outside the school. Carly cried during the entire ceremony, as did Ray. Jake just stood there watching.

Carly returns to her home while Ray, Jake, and Elsie return to the farmhouse. Carly goes inside and runs her a bath. While the bathwater was running, Carly sits at her desk scribbling on her notepad. She undresses, grabs her glass of wine, and gets into the bath. She has a razor blade lying on the floor near the tub. She grabs it and cuts her arm, hitting her bronchial artery. Her arm bleeds out into the water.

The next day, one of her co-workers is knocking on her door. No one answers. They notice that her car is in the driveway. They call the cops. The cops come to the house. The door isn't locked when they check and they walk in. They find Carly in the bathtub deceased.

The cops find the note on Carly's desk. She tells everyone to forgive her but the pain is too great from losing Tate. They notify Ray of Carly's death. Ray is devastated. Jake just looks on as he sees his father fall to his knees from grief. Elsie runs out to see what is wrong. She kneels down to console her son. Jake walks back into the house.

Carly is buried three days later. Ray buries her next to Tate. Jake is angry. He's mad at his mother for what she did. When the family returns home, Jake takes off. He gets in his father's Chevelle and drives down the road. He ends up at one of his friend's houses. His friend is having a party. Jake drinks alcohol and is doing cocaine with one of his good buddies, Will.

Jake meets up with Stephanie Rollins, a girl who is a year younger than him. She's from across the county line and goes to a different school than he does. They leave together. Jake is driving her down one of the country dirt roads with plans of getting lucky. They stop at one of the bends near the creek. They get out of the car and walk along the creekbed.

They're holding hands, talking during their walk along the creekbed. Jake grabs Stephanie and holds her tight. He's kissing her forcefully. Stephanie tries to pull away but he grabs her tighter. She's trying to fight him but she loses. He kicks her foot out from under her and she falls onto the rocks and pebbles below. He gets on top of her, she's still kicking and screaming. He grabs a rock nearby and hits her in the head with it. She's unconscious. He rapes her. When he's done, he drags her to the creek and drowns her. He leaves her there. He heads home.

Stephanie's body floats down the creek. Her parents have called all her friends trying to find her. None of her friends know where she is and hasn't seen her since school the day before. They call the cops to try and report her missing. The cops tell them they have to wait until she's gone for 48 hours. Stephanie is sixteen years old.

Once the 48 hours are up, Stephanie's mother reports her missing. There is an amber alert that goes out to the local newspaper and media stations. Jake is at school and hears everyone talking about the missing girl. He tunes it out and goes about his day normally.

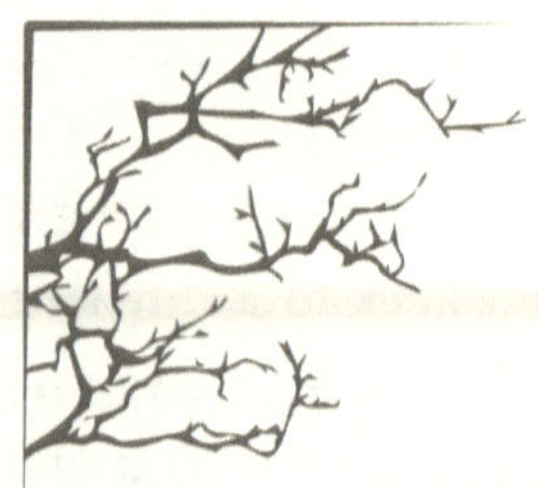

Chapter 4

A week passes before a fisherman discovers a body on the creek. He leaves and drives to the nearest payphone. He phones the police and tells them there's a body on the edge of the water on the other side of the creek. He drives back to his fishing spot. He wants to be there to show the police.

The police arrive fifteen minutes later. They pull the body out of the water and onto a boat. They take the fisherman's statement and make him leave the area. They get the body back to shore. The medical examiner examines the remains before the body is put into a body bag for transport.

The body is taken to the medical examiner's office where an autopsy will be performed. The police look at the body and determine that it's the missing girl, Stephanie. They notify her parents. After the autopsy is performed the medical examiner lists her death as an accident. He believes that she was walking upstream where the creek is rockier, trying to cross, fell and hit her head, and drowned. Stephanie's parents are devastated. Her funeral is four days later.

Jake is now a junior in high school. He is now addicted to drugs. His school work suffers. He skips school almost every day. He spends most of his time with his friend, Will. His teachers try to give him another chance and feel that he's been through a lot with the deaths of his brother and mother. His father is called to the school almost every week.

Ray is working in the field one day close to the end of summer. He's driving his tractor bailing hay. He starts having chest pains. He falls over in the seat of the tractor. Elsie is in the barn shoveling hay for the horses. She looks out the bar door and sees Ray slumped over. She runs to him. He's unresponsive. She runs back to the farmhouse and calls an ambulance.

The ambulance arrives ten minutes later. Ray's breathing and heartbeat are shallow. His blood pressure is high. They suspect he's had a heart attack. They load him on the gurney and take him to the hospital. Elsie gets in her truck and follows. Jake isn't at home. Elsie isn't sure where he is.

Ray is given medicine intravenously to help stabilize his heart and blood pressure. They do an angiogram on him and find several of his arteries blocked. He's taken to the operating room for emergency bypass surgery. The surgery takes hours. Elsie keeps calling the farmhouse hoping Jake is there and answers. She tries over and over but no answer. After eight long hours, the operation was over. The surgeon comes and talks to Elsie and tells her that Ray is in recovery. He tells her that she should go home and get some rest. Elsie stays at the hospital.

Ray is taken to a recovery room. His gown is slightly pulled down on his chest. Elsie sees the staples that hold his surgical wound closed. He's still on the ventilator and asleep. Elsie uses the phone in the room to try the farmhouse again. She's getting furious that she can't get a hold of Jake.

Jake is at his friend Will's house. He's using drugs and drinking whiskey. He eventually passes out. The following morning he wakes up. He's groggy. He gets in the Chevelle and drives home.

Elsie has been trying all night to get a hold of Jake. Ray is now awake in his hospital room. She tries again and this time Jake answers. Elsie is yelling at him telling him that his father is in the hospital. She's upset because she has tried all night to get a hold of him. His father needs him as does she.

He gets in his car and drives to the hospital. He arrives thirty minutes after his grandmother hangs up the phone. When he gets to the room, Elsie smacks him across the face. Jake just looks at her and walks over to his father's bed. Jake apologizes for not being there to help.

Ray is in the hospital for two weeks recovering from his surgery. Jake and Elsie tend to the farm during his recovery. Jake drops out of school. When he's done with the day's farm work he goes to Will's. On weekends he spends his time partying. During those parties, he has sex with different girls. One of the girls is Sadie Hawthorne.

Sadie Hawthorne is the eighteen-year-old daughter of Maude Clemmons. She has long beautiful brown hair, green eyes, and a heart-shaped face. Her home life is difficult. Her father died in an automobile accident when she was ten years old. Maude has always worked and rarely spent time with Sadie after her father's death. Sadie would come home from school and fix her own meals. She would even have to get herself up in the morning and get dressed for school. She is independent. She graduates high school and starts working at the local supermarket. She goes to parties on the weekends to blow off some steam.

JAKE AND SADIE START dating. Sadie eventually moves into the farmhouse with Jake, Ray, and Elsie. She helps Elsie out with the house chores and shoveling hay for the horses. She still works her shifts at the supermarket bringing home income.

She stops going to parties and has applied to the local community college. She wants to get a degree in office administration. The community college offers a two-year bachelor's program for students. She starts college in the fall. Jake isn't happy about her decision but he keeps his feelings to himself. He shows her that he's supportive.

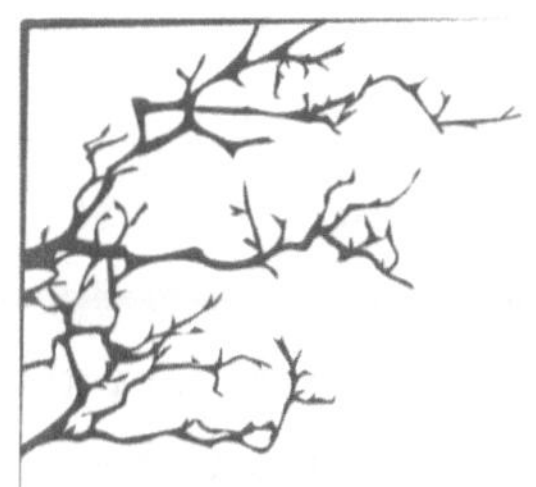

Chapter 5

Sadie dusts the pictures in the living room. She wonders who some of the people are in the photographs. One day she asks Elsie. Elsie tells her who each person in the picture is. She tells Sadie about her parents, grandparents, and great-grandparents, all of whom are in the photographs. Then she starts talking about the one with Ray, Carly, Tate, and Jake. It's a family photo they had made the Christmas before Tate's death. Carly has never heard of Tate. She asks Elsie about Tate and Elsie tells her that he died five years prior.

Sadie mentions to Elsie how beautiful Carly is and asks about her. Elsie tells her that she passed four years ago. Sadie knew Jake's mother was dead but she never knew about his brother Tate. He never talks much about himself unless it's to brag about something he's done.

One night, Jake is drinking at his friend's house. Sadie is at the college doing night classes. Jake has his father's 1972 Chevelle. One of the guys at the party wants to race him. Jake brags that his car will beat the other guys' 1992 Ford Thunderbird. They make a bet on it.

Jake is ready to beat the braggart. They're racing down one of the long paved stretches of roads in their county. They both take off and Jake is ahead. The front tire on the Chevelle blows a mile down the road. Jake loses control and the car hits a tree dead-on. His friend Will calls for help after seeing the crash.

Jake is taken to the hospital. He has a broken arm and concussion. Elsie and Ray were called after it happened. Jake is asleep in the bed when they arrive. Sadie is also notified and rushes to the hospital to be by his side. The police come into the room and cuffs Jake's wrist to the bed. Ray asks them why. They tell him that Jake was drunk when he was driving. They also explain to Ray that he was drag racing in his car. Ray is stunned, upset, and heartbroken. His red beautiful Chevelle was now totaled. He's had that car since high school. He's glad that Jake will be alright though.

Sadie misses two days of school and sits with Jake at the hospital. She is heartsick at the thought that she almost lost him. The doctor plans on releasing him the following day. His wrist is still cuffed to the hospital bed and a police officer is stationed outside his room. When he's released he will be charged with drinking and driving and drag racing. He'll be released on bond and go home.

Jake is in court a month later for his charges. The judge is lenient on him, giving him probation and a fine. Jake pays the fine before leaving the courthouse. Sadie is there with him and they hold hands and smile while exiting the building. Sadie is happy that he didn't get sentenced too harshly.

Two weeks later, they are back at the courthouse. They have filed for a marriage license and hired a justice of the peace to marry them. They return the license after the ceremony for it to be filed. They head out to one of the casinos in the area and spend money on slots and card games. They're both drinking and inebriated. They get the honeymoon suite at the hotel.

Sadie is back at school on Monday. Jake is helping his father with the farm. His grandmother celebrated their spur-of-the-moment wedding with a cake and dinner after they arrived home Sunday. Sadie told her mother, who congratulated her and Jake both.

Even though they were married, Jake still would go to parties at Will's, doing drugs and drinking. One weekend, Sadie was helping Elsie in the kitchen. Ray was in the barn working. Elsie was washing dishes and collapses to the floor. Sadie calls out to Elsie and tries to feel for a pulse. She runs to the phone on the wall and calls an ambulance. She runs back over to Elsie and starts performing CPR on her. Ray has now entered the house through the kitchen door and runs over to his mother. He is freaking out. Sadie tries to keep him calm.

The ambulance arrives and Sadie is still performing CPR. The paramedics check for a pulse. They can't find one. They pull out their paddles and shock her. Her body bounces. They still don't have a pulse. They load her up on the gurney. A paramedic climbs on top, performing CPR as she is wheeled out of the house. Ray and Sadie are upset and crying. They both run to the truck and follow the ambulance to the hospital.

Ray and Sadie rush into the entrance to the Emergency Room. Elsie already arrived and was wheeled in at the ambulance entrance. The paramedics have been working on her the entire trip, trying to revive her. When she is seen at the ER the doctor declared her dead. He goes to the waiting room to tell Ray and Sadie. Ray breaks down. It's been six years of loss and heartbreak for him. Now his 83-year-old mother, the rock that's been keeping him going through all the difficult times is gone.

Ray rushes out of the emergency room entrance and gets in the truck. Sadie runs after him. He speeds out of the parking lot. He goes to Will's house. He walks inside the house looking for his son. Sadie is also looking. He's not there. They can't find him. Will tells Ray that he left an hour ago and didn't know where he was going. They leave and drive home, looking to see if he's walking on the side of the road. They don't find him.

Sadie calls around trying to locate Jake. She has no luck in finding him. Ray heads upstairs and goes to bed. Sadie falls asleep on the couch waiting for Jake to get home.

Jake left Will's with Angela. He spent the night with Angela, drinking and using drugs. They have sex all night. He wakes up the next morning with her by his side. They have sex again and Angela runs to the kitchen to get them both a beer. Jake stays the weekend with Angela. This isn't their first time together. He stays with her most weekends when he doesn't come home. Sadie just thinks that he's camped out at Will's drinking.

Since Jake wrecked the Chevelle he doesn't have a vehicle of his own to drive. Sadie has her Ford Tempo that she drives back and forth to school and work. She won't let Jake drive it. She doesn't want him drinking and driving because if he gets caught within the year, he'll go to jail.

Ray wakes up and goes out to the barn. He has work that needs to be done. Sadie is still asleep on the couch when he trudges through, waking her up. She looks around but sees no sign of Jake anywhere. She's beginning to worry.

Jake makes it home Sunday evening. Sadie asks him where he's been and he lies to her telling her he was at Will's. Sadie tells him she knows he wasn't at Will's because she and his father went looking for him after his grandmother died. Jake is shocked. His grandmother is dead. No wonder she's mad at him. Ray walks up and talks to him, yelling at him for being gone.

Jake goes inside with Sadie. His father heads back to the barn. Sadie is still upset, yelling at Jake for lying to her. He smacks her across the face, knocking her down to the floor. He grabs her by her shirt collar and forces her up the stairs to their bedroom. He continues his assault on her. He punches and slaps her, telling her to never ask him again where he's been and that he'll do whatever he wants. He threatens her, telling her that he would kill her like he has others if she went back to school.

He gets on top of her and chokes her, releasing her before she passes out. Sadie is kicking and screaming the entire time. She is fighting him to get him off of her. Ray can't hear, he's on his tractor in the field. Jake tells her that if she goes to the cops or tells anyone, he'll gut her like a fresh-killed deer.

Sadie sees the look in his eyes and knows he's telling the truth. She starts crying and pleading with him. He walks out of the room and goes downstairs. He's in the kitchen making himself a sandwich when she finally gets down the stairs. Her face is bloodied, bruised and it hurts. Jake yells at her to get back to their bedroom. He didn't want to see her for the rest of the day.

Sadie does as she's told. She heads upstairs. She uses the phone in her bedroom and calls the cops. She isn't going to let this man physically assault her. She knows he said he would kill her and she knows he meant it. She's scared.

The Sheriff arrives ten minutes later. Jake asks him why he was there and they tell him that someone called in an assault. Jake tells the officer that no one has been assaulted there. Ray gets off his tractor once he sees the sheriff's vehicle and walks to the house. Ray tells them he knows nothing about an assault. Sadie makes her way downstairs. She stays in the background without Jake knowing she's there. The Sheriff and his deputy both see her and the condition of her face.

The deputy walks past Jake and Ray to Sadie. Jake is now fuming. The Sheriff grabs Jake's arm and Jake turns around and punches him. Ray is also hit and falls to the ground. He hits his head on the corner of the dining room table. The Sheriff also falls to the ground. Jake runs out the door and into the field. The deputy checks on the sheriff and Ray. Ray is unresponsive and calls for an ambulance. The sheriff is a little woozy from the punch but gathers himself up quickly. They call in for backup to try and catch Jake.

The ambulance arrives and checks on Ray. He's dead. When he fell he hit his temple on the corner of the table and it killed him instantly. Sadie is crying. The paramedics come and check her out. They load her on the gurney to take her to the hospital. The sheriff is waiting for the coroner to come and get Ray.

Sadie's injuries from Jake's assault are documented. Jake still hasn't been caught by the police. They are even doing air searches for him. Ray's body is taken to the morgue.

After the examination, Sadie gets a washcloth from the bathroom and runs water over it. She's cleaning her blood-soaked face, neck, and hands. She gets out of her blood-stained clothes and turns on the shower. She gets in and washes her body. Her face stings when the water hits it. When she gets out and looks in the mirror, she can see marks on her neck from where his hands choked her. Her right eye is busted and swelling. She has a cut on her chin.

Her clothes are put in an evidence bag and she is given sweat pants and a t-shirt to put on. She is released shortly after. Her mother is there to pick her up from the hospital. She doesn't want to go to her mother's house and asks if there is a shelter nearby to stay at until they catch Jake. They give her directions to the shelter and her mother drops her off.

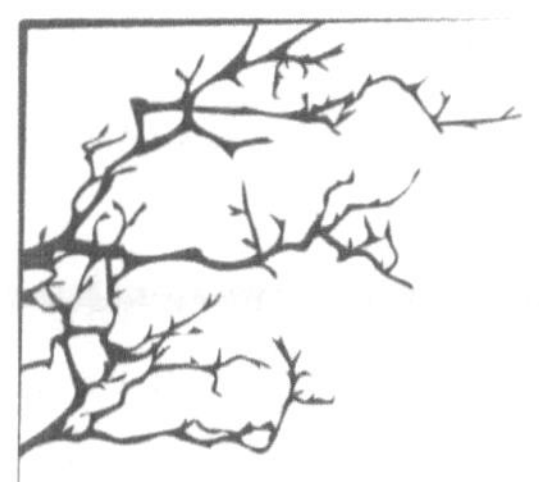

Chapter 6

Jake ran from the farmhouse to an underground bunker outside of the farm. He has been staying there for a week now. The police have exhausted their search of the area. Sadie is staying at the shelter, missing college and work. She is scared to go outside. She's scared Jake will find her.

When the sheriff spoke to Sadie she told him what Jake had told her about how he would kill her like he's done others. She didn't know what he meant by it but knew he wasn't lying. The sheriff just gazes off for a second, thinking about what she just said.

After Sadie's statement, the sheriff looks into Tate's death. He wasn't a sheriff at the time but remembers the case. He was one of the responding officers on the scene. He remembers how Jake acted when no one was looking. He would have a smirk on his face. Once he noticed someone was looking at him his expression would change. The sheriff grabs the file and goes to talk to the previous sheriff about it.

The file didn't have a statement in it from Jake. The sheriff just assumed it was an accident and that Jake was in shock from it. There were no witnesses to the shooting as his parents and grandmother were in the kitchen and came out after hearing the shot. He told them that the gun was on the floor when they arrived, stating that the father had removed it from Jake's hands after the shooting.

Ray did tell the sheriff that Jake had the gun pointed in the direction of Tate but that after they ran in there he lowered it toward the floor. He thought it was a little strange but also thought maybe it was because of the kickback action of the rifle. He also didn't understand why Jake was standing when he was sitting and cleaning the gun when he walked into the kitchen. Ray also stated that he made sure the rifle was unloaded before handing it to Jake to clean. Ray wasn't irresponsible, he was a former Marine.

The sheriff didn't have enough to charge Jake with the death of Tate. The coroner ruled it an accidental shooting. Elsie even backed up the story about the family being in the kitchen and the two boys in the living room. She didn't know that Jake was cleaning the rifle. When she walked into the living room he was standing up with the barrel pointed down toward the floor looking at his brother. To her, he had a look of dismay.

When the sheriff goes back to the office, he looks at Carly's suicide. She killed herself because her son Tate was gone. If Jake was truly responsible for Tate's death, he would also be responsible for his mother's death. He already knew he was guilty of his father's death. His father wouldn't be dead if he hadn't punched them.

The sheriff heads to the shelter to talk to Sadie. He explains to her what happened to Tate. Sadie didn't know about it. She told the sheriff that Jake never even mentioned a brother and she didn't find out until Elsie had told her. She only knew that Jake's mother was dead but she didn't know how she died. She just assumed it was a car accident like the one that killed her father. Sadie was shocked. Could Jake actually be responsible?

Jake calls Angela and tells her to come to get him. He meets her down the road from his house. He gets in the trunk and tells her to drive to her house. She does as he says. The police have a roadblock up. They're looking at the drivers to see if any of them are Jake. Angela stops and they do a quick look over her vehicle. They let her pass.

When she arrives home, she pulls her car into the garage. She opens the trunk and Jake gets out. He wants them to leave together and move to Vegas. Over the next week, they sell all of her household items and pack up to go to Vegas. Angela has always wanted to live in Vegas. She wants to be a showgirl.

Angela and Jake drive the twelve-hour trip to Vegas and get a room for the night. Tomorrow they will look for an apartment and a job. Jake tells Angela that he's gonna have to change his name. They look online through the obituaries and find one. His name would now be Joshua James.

He gets a new social security card and birth certificate delivered to him by FedEx. He uses them to get a driver's license issued. Afterward, he applies for jobs. Within a week he is working as a security guard at one of the casinos in Vegas. Angela got a job as a server at the same casino. She makes good money from tips.

They find an apartment to rent and move in. They buy new furniture and furnish it. They have also found a drug dealer in the area to get drugs from. When they aren't working they snort cocaine up their noses and drink the night away. Within a month they are Vegans.

Sadie has started back to her on-campus classes. She has also gone back to her job. Her face is almost fully healed and she uses concealer to hide what's still there. The police have no idea where Jake is. They suspect he's no longer in the area. Sadie filed for a quick divorce. It was granted. Now she's no longer married to Jake.

Elsie's estate pays for her and Ray's burials. Since Sadie and Jake are still married, Sadie can live on the farm if she wants. She refuses. She decides to put it up for sale. She knows that Jake will go to jail when he's caught so she'll inherit it either way. She meets a local realtor at the farmhouse. She doesn't know what she wants for it so the realtor tells her its value. Sadie still has to meet with an attorney and get the paperwork in order but tells the realtor it shouldn't take long.

The paperwork for the farm has been transferred to Sadie's name. She is the last living survivor besides Jake who's on the run from the cops. Sadie tells the realtor to put the farm up for sale since all of the paperwork is now in order.

Sadie has an estate sale and sells the farm animals. She also sells the tractor. She has already accumulated over two hundred thousand dollars just from those sales. Now she is selling all other household items. She boxes up the personal items of Elsie and Ray including the pictures.

By the time the estate sale is over, Sadie has made close to three hundred thousand dollars. She puts the money in her banking account. Now she has to wait for the house and farm to sell.

Two months later and the farm was sold. Sadie makes a million dollars from the sale. She deposits it into her checking account. She graduates from college and applies for jobs. She isn't planning on staying in her hometown.

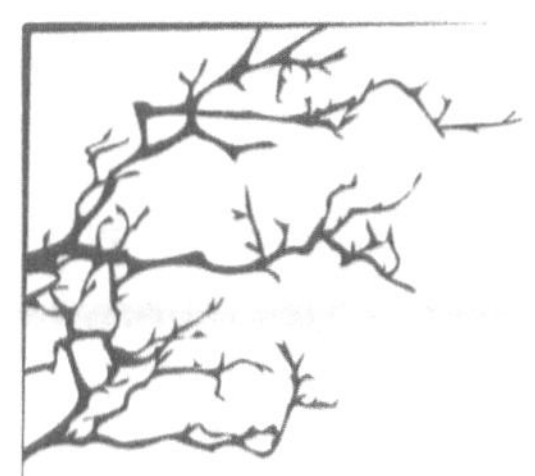

Chapter 7

Sadie stored Elsie and Ray's personal items in her garage. She wants to keep them and show her child when they're older. Sadie is four months pregnant. The child is Jake's. She's going to do her best to make sure he never knows of the child.

Jake and Angela are living the high life in Vegas. Both of them are making good money. Since Jake has changed his name, he thinks he can legally marry Angela. They go to one of the wedding chapels on the Las Vegas strip and get married. Their friends from work are there to cheer them on. They take a small honeymoon to Hawaii. They return two days later ready to get back to work.

Sadie got a job opportunity in Seattle, Washington. She and her mother pack up the Uhaul and hitch the Ford Tempo and leave their old lives behind. The trip is hard on Sadie. She has to stop and pee quite often from the baby pushing down on her bladder. What should've been a twenty-hour drive turned into a forty-hour drive. Sadie and Maude would take turns driving the Uhaul. They also stopped to rest at night.

Sadie had already bought a home for her, her mom, and the baby. It's near where she'll be working. It's supposed to be in a good, friendly, and safe neighborhood. They arrive shortly after dark and park in the drive. Sadie and her mother go inside and look around. It's partially furnished and Sadie collapses on the bed. She's exhausted from the drive. She suddenly feels the urge to pee. She has trouble getting up from the bed but finally is able to and makes her way to the bathroom.

Maude is in the other room and falls asleep. Sadie leaves the bathroom and lies back down. It isn't long until she's fast asleep.

Morning comes and the movers have arrived to unload the Uhaul. They unhook the car from the hitch and raise the door to the truck. It wakes Sadie up, startling her. She looks out the window and sees the movers. She runs to the other room and wakes up her mother. They both go outside to the truck.

The movers get everything inside and set up in five hours. They take the Tempo off the hauler and park it in the garage. They hitch the hauler back on the truck and drive it to the nearest dealer. Sadie has paid them for their help. Now she has to get the rest of her life in order before the baby arrives.

Maude takes the Tempo and trades it for a Ford Windstar. Sadie goes along and purchases a Ford Taurus. They drive the vehicles home and store them in the double garage. Sadie schedules an appointment with an OB/GYN for Monday. She has a week to get everything organized before starting work the following Monday.

The new doctor checks Sadie out thoroughly. She even performs an ultrasound. She asks Sadie if she wants to know the gender and she tells her yes. The doctor discloses that it's a girl. When she arrives home, she tells her mother the news. They decide to go baby shopping.

The following day Sadie and Maude go to the DMV to change their driver's license to Washington State. Now she has to stop by the office she'll be working at and give them copies of her new driver's license, and social security card, and fill out paperwork. The people are nice to her and she feels at home.

Jake and Angela are partying again on their usual Saturday evening. Angela can't party like usual because she has to work the following day. Jake makes her a drink and hands it to her. She drinks it and starts feeling woozy. She goes and lies down on the bed. Jake leaves once she's asleep.

Jake heads to his new friend, Sally's apartment. They continue partying and eventually have sex. He stays there until the morning. He returns to his apartment and finds Angela still asleep. Her alarm goes off two hours later and she starts to stir. Jake is asleep beside her. She gets ready for work. She leaves the apartment and heads to work.

Jake wakes up a few hours later and heads back over to Sally's. She opens the door and they kiss as he walks inside. One of their friends sees the lip exchange. They go to the casino where Angela is working and tell her. She leaves work and returns home. Jake is not at home. She sits and waits for him to return. He doesn't. She goes and knocks on Sally's door. No one answers.

Jake returns home shortly after two in the morning. Angela had been waiting for him all evening. He walks in the door and the apartment is dark. He guesses Angela is asleep. He turns on the light and she is sitting on a chair in front of the television. Her arms are crossed and she's fuming. She gets up and starts yelling at him, asking him where he's been. She knows he's out cheating on her.

While she is in his face yelling at him, he balls his fist up and punches her. She starts screaming. He continues hitting her. She is screaming and crying. He grabs a lamp from the table and smashes it over her head continuously. She isn't moving. He bends down and puts his head on her chest. She isn't breathing and he doesn't hear her heart beating. He gets up and leaves. He returns to Sally's apartment.

He stays at Sally's apartment for two days. He doesn't return home. One of Angela's friends comes over to the apartment to check on her. She unlocks the door and finds Angela laying in a pool of blood. She screams a blood-curdling scream and runs out of the apartment.

Jake hears the screams from inside Sally's apartment. He casually tells Sally he has to go to work and leaves. He walks down the stairs and gets into Sally's car and drives off. He parks the car in a parking garage. He grabs his jacket and walks away. He soon finds an unoccupied car and the keys are in the ignition. He gets in it and drives off.

He makes his way down west. He's heading for Los Angeles, California. He cleaned out their safe before he left and has thousands of dollars in his pocket. The cops put out an APB for Angela's husband,

Joshua James. They even added a picture to the newspapers and media. It was their wedding picture. The story made national headlines.

Sadie was looking through the newspaper and came across a gruesome story of a woman beaten to death in her home. She sees the picture of the happy couple and recognizes the groom. It's her ex-husband Jake. He had been living in Las Vegas. She calls the Vegas police and tells them what she knows about the man in the paper who's known as Joshua James. She tells them to contact the sheriff back home to confirm what she is saying.

The next day she looks in the paper and sees a new story with the correct name of the perpetrator. The story details the gruesome murder of Angela James at her apartment, the death of his father, and the physical assault on her. It even says that he's wanted in several states for violent crimes and to be on the lookout for him. It also states that he's extremely dangerous.

Jake has made his way to Los Angeles. Once he's checked into his hotel room he tries to find a new identity to take. He can't find any obituaries. There usually aren't many twenty-two-year-olds who pass away. Jake decides to take a walk. He exits the hotel and starts walking down the street.

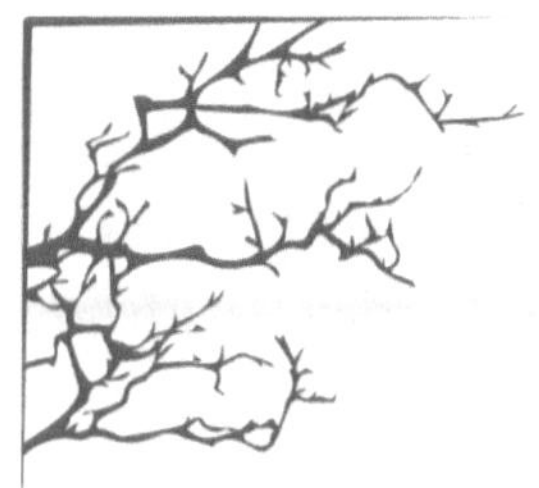

Chapter 8

The Las Vegas police happen upon Sally. They ask her questions regarding Joshua a.k.a. Jake. At the time they didn't know his actual name. She tells them that Josh was with her all weekend and never left the apartment. She tells them that she and Josh had been secretly dating for months now.

Sally also tells them that he went to work a couple of hours ago. They discover that he isn't at the casino where he works. She goes downstairs to drive to the store and realizes that her car is gone. She calls the police to report it stolen.

The police find her car in a parking garage near one of the many casinos. They impound it and look over it. Sally was maybe 5'3" and the driver's seat was further back than what it would have been for Sally. They suspect that Josh had taken it without her knowledge.

They make their way through the casinos showing his picture but no one has seen him. They try to look at security footage from the garage but find that there isn't any. The cameras haven't been working for months now.

After looking through the crime scene, they find bloody fingerprints all over the lamp that was used to hit Angela. They run them through AFIS and no hits come back. They keep them on file. They suspect Josh is the one who killed his wife Angela and decide to use the media to help find him.

Sadie is adjusting to her new life. She's happy that her mother is with her and able to share the new life. She understood why her mother was always away when she was a teenager. It was hard for them after her father died. Her mother can also take it easy now that Sadie has money.

During Jake's walk through the city streets, he happens upon a homeless community. There are tents put up under an overpass. He watches as the members interact with others. He sees someone he thinks is special. He tries to figure out a way to make friends with him. He follows the guy for days, watching his every move, trying to figure out how to make friends with him.

On the second day, he decides to try and buy the man some food and get to know him better. He uses a ruse, explaining to the young man that he has millions of dollars and owns a company that is looking for someone savvy to work. Of course, Jake isn't a millionaire or owns a company. It's his way of trying to get the man to trust him.

While they eat and talk, Jake realizes he'll make a perfect replacement for him. He looks similar to Jake. He's dirty and his hair is long but Jake thinks he can make him look closer to him. He and the young man take off in Jake's stolen car. They stop at one of the industrial areas. Jake and the young man go inside.

Jake has a .45 pistol on him, concealed by his jacket. While the young man, James Waters, is walking in front of him, Jake pulls the pistol out and aims it at the back of James' head, and shoots. James falls to the ground. Jake looks through James' clothes and finds his wallet. He looks through the wallet and puts it in his pocket and runs back to his vehicle.

He goes back to the hotel. He collects his belongings and throws them in the backseat of the car and drives off. He's heading south to San Diego. He plans on renting an apartment there and holding up for a while using the dead man's identity.

Jake's plan goes off without a hitch. He immediately finds a furnished apartment and pays two months' rent. He begins looking for a job and finds one as a car detailer. This is when he meets Jaden Phillips.

Jaden is a nineteen-year-old woman who works at Shine and Sparkle, the car detailer. She helps detail the vehicles that come through the shop. She and Jake hit it off almost immediately. They start dating. Within a few months, they are living together.

Sadie is now at her six months appointment for her baby, Hannah Leigh, the name she and Maude came up with. They have gotten the nursery furnished with the name across the wall. They painted the walls a light pink color. They used small pink colored stripes of wallpaper to cover the bottom quarter of the wall. Between the wallpaper and the paint, they use a white strip of board to divide them. They add pink stuffed animals, diapers, wipes, and all essentials for the baby. They wash and dry the baby clothes in perfume and dye-free detergent and fold and hang them after. The room is almost ready.

Maude brings in the old rocking chair she used when Sadie was an infant. She sanded it and repainted it. She even added a design on the top of it. The rocking chair will now have been through three generations of the Hawthorne family.

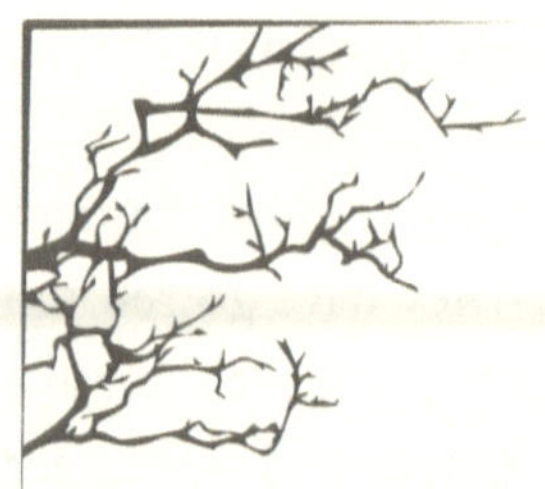

Chapter 9

Maude got pregnant when she was seventeen years old after being raped during an attack while walking home from school. Her mother saw her when she got home that day. She was disheveled and her knees were bleeding. Maude never saw the person who attacked her and she never spoke about her rape to Sadie.

When she found out she was pregnant, she told her mother what had happened. They kept it a secret from her father for months. Maude had been dating a boy from school, Jared Hawthorne but they never had intercourse during the courtship.

She was barely able to graduate high school before Sadie was born. Maude cherished her new baby girl. Jared was by her side when Sadie was born. Maude had told him what had happened. Two months after Sadie's birth her mother and Jared marry. Jared has a good job with a local car dealership, selling brand new Fords. He, Maude, and Sadie all move into a home together and become a family.

Maude and Jared's relationship was normal. Jared would ride bulls in high school and during one of the rides, he got bucked off and the bull stepped on him. The bull's hoof squashed Jared's testes. He wasn't able to have children. He knew that Sadie would be their only child and he spoiled her.

He would bring her a gift home every day when he came home from work. It could've been a small stuffed animal or a coloring book. He stopped at the five and dime near the dealership and bought her something. Sadie would color in the coloring books until every page was colored. He would even buy the small books that helped her learn to write. She mastered writing before even starting kindergarten.

Jared had left work for the day when he was t-boned in the driver's side of the car after a man ran a red light. He was killed instantly. During his lunch break that day he had stopped at the five and dime store and had bought a barbie doll for Sadie. Her mother found it in the wreckage when she went to clean the car out before it was taken to the recycling yard to be crushed. Maude gave it to her daughter and Sadie kept it in its box all these years. She stores it on a shelf in her room so she can remember the last thing her father ever gave her.

Two years after her father's death, Maude started dating Jack Clemmons. They married a few months later. After two years of marriage, they divorce. Jack had been cheating on Maude for the duration of the marriage. He was an office manager and had been in a relationship with his secretary for almost two years.

After the divorce is when Maude started working all the time. Sadie had to become independent and take care of herself. She was fourteen years old then. She taught herself how to cook and even made a plate for her mother to eat when she got home from work. Maude had always been appreciative toward Sadie. They didn't have a close-knit relationship they had before, it was just different now. Sadie loved her mother, she cherished her. When she was sixteen she found a job until her grades started slipping and Maude made her quit. Sadie graduated from high school as an honor student.

Maude had worked hard for two decades providing for Sadie. At times, she would wake up with her hands asleep and hurting from the carpal tunnel. She would cry from the pain. The doctors wanted to put her on pain medicine but she refused. She would wear a brace at night while sleeping. It helped some.

Sadie wanted to help her mother and when she got the money from the estate, she talked her mother into moving away. Maude sold her two-bedroom home for fifty-five grand and put the money in her account. She moved with Sadie to Washington. She cleans the house while Sadie works. She takes breaks watching her soap operas and game shows.

She plans on babysitting Hannah when it's time for Sadie to return to work after her birth. She has set up a playpen, swing, and bouncer in the living room to keep her nearby while she cleans during the day.

Chapter 10

It's three in the morning. Sadie wakes up to a warm, wet spot on the bed. She is in pain. She yells out in pain. Maude comes running to her room to see what's going on. Sadie has three weeks left in her pregnancy. Her water has broken all over the mattress. Maude grabs the overnight bag that has been packed for weeks and runs it downstairs to the van. She opens the garage door before running back upstairs to help Sadie down the stairs and to the van.

Sadie is panting with the contractions. She waddles slowly down the stairs. Halfway down the stairs, a contraction comes. She sits down on the step and waits for it to pass. Maude is talking to her through her breathing. When the contraction is over she stands and walks down the stairs. They get to the kitchen and another contraction happens. Sadie grabs the island's edge. Maude is concerned. The contractions are close together.

Maude puts her arm around Sadie and they make it to the van. Sadie gets in the passenger seat and Maude runs around the front of the van and gets in the driver's seat. She starts the van and leaves the garage, hitting the garage opener on her way out. She turns down the neighborhood street and rushes toward the hospital.

It's the rainy season in Seattle. Maude drives carefully, trying to miss the puddles and not hydroplaning. Sadie's contractions are less than two minutes apart. Maude makes it to the hospital in less than fifteen minutes. She goes to the passenger side and helps Sadie out of the van. Sadie is hurting. She tells her mother that it's time. Maude rushes in and tells them they need help. A nurse runs out to the van. Sadie is lying on the concrete walkway.

The baby's head has crowned. The nurse removes Sadie's underwear and she delivers baby Hannah there, on the sidewalk, outside the emergency room. After the baby is delivered, Sadie and the baby are rushed inside on a gurney. They are taken upstairs to the maternity ward. Hannah is crying. They put her in a warmer. She will soon be cleaned and everything checked to make sure she is healthy. Sadie has to wait until her placenta is delivered, which doesn't take long.

Sadie and Hannah are both doing well. They will be released the next day. Maude stays at the hospital until both are checked out and cleared of any complications. She kisses both of them and returns home.

Jaden has fallen in love with James a.k.a. Jake. Jake uses her love for him to take advantage of her. He makes her feel guilty when she doesn't do something he wants until she does and then he makes her feel loved. Jaden is young and doesn't realize that Jake is mentally abusing her.

Jake bought a promise ring for Jaden. He surprises her with it one evening. She is ecstatic. She thinks he's proposing to her. He realizes what she is thinking and proposes to her using the promise ring. He doesn't love her the way she loves him. He's incapable of love. She doesn't know that though. She's happy and willing to do anything for him.

One night, she makes dinner for the two of them. She adds candles to the table and sets the table up for romance. She wants to show Jake how much she loves and cares about him. He arrives home and they sit and eat dinner. Jaden had been sick for weeks, throwing up. She went to the doctor and found out she was pregnant. She tells Jake over dinner about the baby. He pretends he's happy about the pregnancy but inside he's furious.

After dinner, they go to the bedroom and have intercourse. Shortly after, Jaden falls asleep. Jaden wakes up tied to the bed. Jake has duct-taped her mouth so she can't scream. He's on top of her with a knife to her throat. She's crying out in fear. She tries to speak but it's muffled by the tape. He whispers in her ear that she should've never gotten pregnant. He stabs her repeatedly until she is dead.

Jake takes a shower and changes clothes. He leaves in Jaden's car and heads east. He's making his way toward Phoenix, Arizona. He looks out the windshield and sees miles ahead into the desert land.

James' body is discovered in the warehouse. He is listed as a John Doe. His body is badly decomposed and trying to ID him will be difficult. It's been months since Jake shot and killed him and with the San Diego heat, it sped up the decomposition.

James wasn't listed as a missing person. The coroner's office has tried to run facial recognition through their database after his skull was forensically reconstructed. It's been a week since they started running it and so far no hits. It takes another week before the facial recognition gets a hit. The man is James Waters an army officer that went awol a year earlier. They examine James' clothes and realize that they were torn and tattered. His shoes showed signs of heavy use, meaning that he walked everywhere. They suspect he had been living at one of the homeless camps in the area.

The San Diego police search for answers in the death of James Waters. They know it will be difficult because the homeless usually don't help. Soon the case goes cold and is forgotten about.

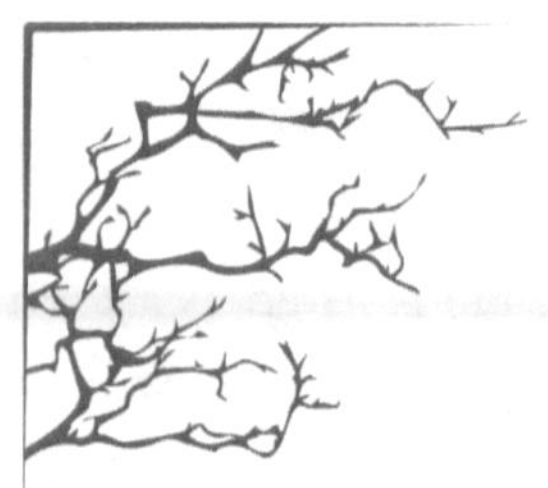

Chapter 11

Jaden and Jake haven't shown up to work in days. Their boss just assumes they quit. Neighbors of the couple keep calling the manager of the apartment building about a foul smell in their apartments. The manager just assumes that it's a dead mouse and ignores it. Days later the smell gets worse and the neighbors call complaining. The manager knocks on the door to Jaden and Jake's apartment and gets no answer. He calls the cops.

The rookie cops have the apartment manager open the door to Jaden and Jake's apartment after they knocked several times with no answer. They walk in and see a gruesome scene. They run out of the apartment to the hallway and call it in to dispatch. One of the officers is hurling in the hallway. The other one stands by the door and waits for the homicide detectives to show up.

The detectives walk inside the apartment and see a body lying on the bed, bound to the bedposts. There is blood everywhere. The medical examiner comes to the scene and looks over the body. There are at least twenty stab wounds to the victim's abdomen, chest and face. Crime scene investigators film the crime scene before the body is removed. The investigators ask for information on the tenant of the apartment from the building manager.

The investigators search through the apartment and find a purse. The ID in the purse belongs to Jaden Phillips, a young female, 19 years of age. They look at pictures in her apartment and find recent ones of her with a young man named James Waters. His name sounds familiar. They do a search and realize that he's a body in their morgue. The picture was dated a couple of weeks ago. They're both standing outside the Shine and Sparkle car detailing shop.

The investigators get finished with the apartment and head over to the shop to ask about Jaden and James. The boss, Samuel, tells the detectives that neither one has been to work since Friday and just assumed they had quit. He didn't know much about James but talked about Jaden. James had only been working for him for about three months. He said that James told him that he came to San Diego from Los Angeles. He didn't know much else and gave the cops a copy of his application.

Jaden had worked at the shop since she was sixteen years old. She had been a sweet, wonderful girl and could run circles around the guys cleaning and detailing the vehicles that came through. She had grown up in the custody of the state and was making plans on going to college next year. She wanted to be a laboratory assistant. Sam was heartbroken after the detectives told him she was deceased.

Jake had made it to Phoenix. He would park in one of the lots and sleep during the night. The next morning he made his way around the city looking for someone similar to him to take over their identity. He finds a young man, Charlie Holman, and mugs him. He takes his wallet after knocking him down to the ground. He runs off before anyone can catch him.

Charlie has hundreds of dollars in his wallet. He has multiple bank cards. Jake isn't interested in the bank cards though and throws them in a trash bin along the sidewalk where he's walking. He takes out his old wallet that belonged to James Waters and takes out the money he has in it and puts it in the new wallet. He discards it in a separate trash bin. He finds a motel nearby and gets a room for the week. He's using Charlie's identification.

A man walks by and looks in the trash bins. He sees the two bank cards and takes them from the trash. He uses them at a bar to open a tab. Charlie had called the police after he was knocked down and his wallet stolen. The cops knew that the person responsible would try to use the cards. They arrive at the bar and arrest Matt Laughlin for the mugging and robbery.

Matt tells the police he found the cards in a trash bin. They don't believe him. He is bonded out by his mother and appears in court in a month. Jake is looking for a job in the city. He comes upon an ad for an insurance salesman. He applies and soon gets the job. He has to walk door to door trying to sell life insurance to customers. Soon he comes to a red brick home. He knocks. A young woman in her early twenties answers.

He starts talking to her about the insurance he offers. She tells him she wasn't interested and he leaves. He jots down the address on his notepad. He makes his way through the lovely neighborhood before calling it a night. He sold two policies.

He buys a car from a used car salesman. He makes monthly payments on it. He uses it for work. He drives back to the neighborhood where the young woman leaves and sits in his car outside the house watching. He watches most of the night. He only sees her coming and going. About three in the morning he gets out of his car and walks around to the back of the house. The back door isn't locked and he goes inside.

He makes his way to the kitchen and grabs a knife from the block and makes his way through the house. He finds the woman asleep in her bed. He creeps into her room and to her bed. He stands there, watching her sleep for a minute or two. He walks slowly to the other side of the bed and gently gets into the bed to not disturb the sleeping young woman. He rolls over and puts his hand over the woman's mouth, waking her. She tries to scream and starts thrashing in the bed, trying to get away and he sticks the knife to her throat and threatens to kill her. She calms down and he grabs the pillowcase from her pillow and ties her hands up behind her back. He grabs a second pillowcase and puts it around her mouth, gagging her. It takes him about three minutes to get her restrained and turned over on her back.

With the knife still to her throat, he uses his free hand and rolls up her nightgown. He moves the knife down to her panties and cuts both sides off of her. She is frozen in fear. He unzips his zipper and inserts his penis inside her roughly. She's screaming through the gag. He cuts her throat during one of his rough thrusts. She is slightly bleeding. He finishes and then cuts her throat, slashing it from ear to ear. She dies moments later.

Jake rummages through the house grabbing money and other valuables before leaving. He gets in his car and drives back to his hotel. His adrenaline is rushing through his body. He is so excited he can't sleep. He grabs a beer from his mini-fridge and drinks it. He's trying to wound down. He finally falls asleep as the sun comes up.

Chapter 12

Sadie and Hannah are released from the hospital. Maude helps Sadie with Hannah. They take turns tending to the baby. Sadie is overjoyed about Hannah. Sadie returns to work when her six-week maternity leave is over. Her co-workers want to see pictures of the baby. She shows one that she brought from home to put in her office. They all give her praise and congratulations on the new baby.

Maude cares for Hannah while Sadie is working. She makes dinner for her and Sadie. She cleans the house and does the laundry. She even takes Hannah with her to shop. Many people look at the beautiful baby in the car seat on the cart and congratulate Maude. Maude tells them that it's her new granddaughter.

One day a man, Michael Blankenship, sees Maude and the baby in the store. He tells her the usual and she explains her story. He quips to her that she looks too young to be a grandmother. They chuckle and talk during the shopping trip. He helps her with her purchases to the van and loads them for her. She puts the baby in the van while he loads up the van. They continue talking and eventually exchange phone numbers.

Maude and Michael are talking on the phone and decide to go out on Saturday evening. Sadie is happy for her mother. She has a date. Sadie takes her mother shopping for a new dress and shoes. She has a spa day with her mother and gets their nails and hair done. Sadie keeps an eye on Hannah who's asleep in her car seat sitting on the floor in front of her chair. She takes a break from the spa activities when Hannah needs her.

After their nails and hair are done, Sadie has the beautician do their make-up. She wants a natural look for her and her mother. The beautician makes their faces look flawless. When they arrive home, there is just enough time for Maude to get dressed for her date with Michael. She changes clothes, puts on her deodorant and perfume, and a pearl necklace, and heads downstairs. Sadie whistles at her mother acceptingly, who blushes.

Michael and Maude go out to a fancy restaurant and talk while they eat dinner. They talk about their lives. Maude tells him she's been married twice, a widow and a divorcee. She tells him that her daughter and granddaughter are her world. He tells her that he's also been married twice and twice divorced. He has a child in college from his first wife. He's an attorney for a big firm. They continue talking and eating. Eventually, the restaurant closes and the wait staff has to tell them it's closing time. They sat there all evening talking. Michael pays and they exit the restaurant.

Michael drives Maude home. He walks her to the door and kisses her good night. They make plans to go out later in the week. Michael will be busy all week in court and when he's home he talks to Maude on the phone. They speak every day.

Sadie starts going to the gym after work. She wants to get rid of the baby weight. She is working with a trainer, Maxwell Sharp. Maxwell is almost thirty years old and teaches various classes at the gym. Maxwell finds Sadie attractive. He tries to ask her out but she keeps turning him down. She isn't ready to start dating. She has a three-month-old daughter at home. Hannah is her life. She isn't going to risk anything by dating anyone.

Jake is working in a different neighborhood in Phoenix on Monday morning. He knocks on a door to a yellow siding house owned by a retired couple. He gives them his sales pitch and they welcome him inside. The retired gentleman asks Jake what his rates are to see if they're any better than the company he's currently with. Jake tells him and he decides to take out a new policy on himself and his wife.

The young woman's body was discovered the day following her death. Her husband had been away for work and arrived home that morning. He found her dead in her room and called the cops. They suspect it was a random burglary. They find a business card on the end table near the couch with the name Charlie Holman etched in gold letters. They put it into evidence not knowing its significance.

Jake turns in his paperwork for the retired couple and heads back out into the neighborhood going door to door. This time he knocks on the door of a home owned by Jennifer Winkle. She is thirty years old and a single mother. Her ex-husband has the kids on the weekends. Jake takes note of the house and the woman.

It's Friday night and Jake is parked outside the Winkle home. He watches as the house turns dark. About three in the morning he gets out of his car and makes his way to the back of the house. He breaks in. He rapes and kills Jennifer. He looks through the house, grabbing money, spare change, and anything of value. He leaves and heads back to his hotel.

Saturday morning he rents a storage unit. He puts some of the stolen items into the storage locker and leaves. Saturday night he drives over to where the retired couple lives. He watches as their house goes dark. He breaks in and kills them both. He stabs them multiple times with a kitchen knife from their kitchen. He loads up their television and other items into the truck in the garage. He looks through their wallet and purse and takes their money. He drives the truck from the garage to the storage locker and unloads the stolen property. He drives the truck back to the house and stores it in the garage. He runs to his parked car and leaves.

The police are called to the home of the retired couple the following day. Their son had come by to check on his parents and discovered them. They search the house and gather evidence. They believe that it is a robbery.

Sunday evening, Jennifer Winkles's ex-husband, Shawn arrives at her home to drop their children off. When he knocks on the door no one answers. He knows where a spare key is hidden and unlocks the door. He tells the two children to stay outside while he goes inside and looks around. He sees the house in disarray and finds Jennifer's dead body in the bedroom. He runs to the neighbor's house with his children and calls 911.

The Phoneix police arrive and the detectives gather up items as evidence. Jennifer's body is photographed and taken to the morgue. The detectives talk to Shawn about his whereabouts over the weekend. Shawn has a new wife who confirms his alibi. He takes his children home with him. Shawn and his children are visibly upset about Jennifer's death.

The Phoenix detectives run the prints from all three murder scenes and get a hit in AFIS to crimes in Las Vegas and San Diego. Their prime suspect now becomes Jake Morris. The detectives decide to work together to find the serial killer. Jake has now killed multiple people in different states. They suspect he will be on the run again. They look through the evidence from the homes of their four victims and discover a commonality. A business card with the name Charlie Holman on it.

The detectives drive to the Holman home to speak with Charlie. He explains to them that he was mugged months earlier and that they arrested a man for it. The detectives ask him about his work as an insurance salesman and Charlie has no idea what they're talking about. He works as an analytical advisor. They show Charlie the business cards and he explains that they weren't his.

The detectives start suspecting that Jake is using an alias. He used several before. They believe he is Charlie Holman the insurance sales agent. They drive to the insurance company that is printed on the cards hoping to find answers. When the detectives arrive at the company office they are greeted by the secretary. They show her their badges and ask to speak to the manager. The manager comes out of his office and shakes their hands. He asks them why they are there and the detectives tell him. He shows them to his office.

The manager tells the officers that Charlie has worked for them for months and that he makes several sales a week. He's one of their best salesmen. The detectives ask to see his application and ask how he gets paid and all other relevant questions to try and find the man named Charlie.

When they leave the office they head out to an address that is on the application. They realize that it's to a hotel. They go inside and show the front desk a picture of Jake and ask if they have seen him. The hotel attendant tells them that the man was there until recently. They didn't know where he went. He checked out and left. The detectives left.

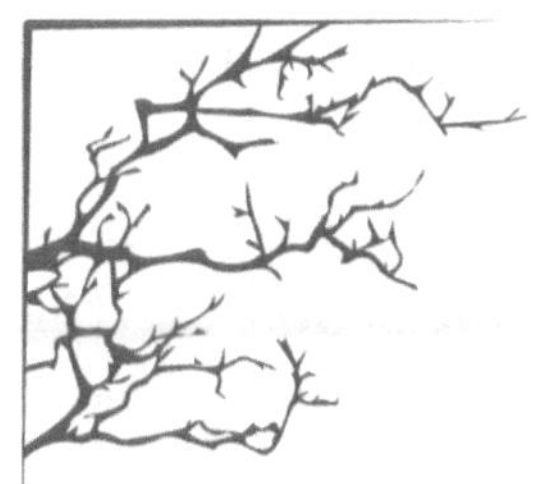

Chapter 13

Jake left Phoenix and his job as a salesman and drove east. He makes his way toward Dallas, Texas. There he meets a woman named Laura Westwood. She is a 25-year-old bartender. He is living in his car. He sold the stolen property from his storage unit before he left to have money. He feels it's too dangerous to get a motel room. He works as a farmhand gathering vegetables. He gets paid cash daily. No one at the farm asks questions. Many of the other farmhands are immigrants or migrant workers.

He goes to the bar every evening to see Laura. He moves in with her after a few weeks. He keeps working as a farmhand. He likes the job. It gives him camouflage. He leaves work every night and goes to the bar. Sometimes it's the one Laura works at and other times it's a different one.

Sadie gets a call from the detectives in Las Vegas. They update her on Jake and his crimes. They ask her if she is willing to help. She tells them that she has to think about it. A reporter for 20/20 has picked up the story of Jake and calls Sadie at home wanting to interview her. Sadie declines.

Sadie talks the idea over with Maude. Hannah is almost a year old. The Vegas detectives call her a week later and have the other detectives on the call with them and they all ask her to help. Sadie calls the reporter back when she gets off the phone and agrees to an interview.

During the interview, Sadie tells the reporter about Jake's life. They show different pictures of Jake on the screen. Sadie tells them about his brother Tate's death and how it was originally ruled an accident. She believes that it was Jake's first murder. She then tells about Jake's mother's suicide and how it came to be. She was depressed after Tate's death and felt she couldn't live without him. She also spoke about how she was a loving mother and nurse at the hospital. She talks about the first time she met Jake and she thought he was the perfect man. He was sweet toward her. She didn't know that he had been seeing other women.

She talked about how they would get drunk on the weekends until she went back to college. He continued partying on the weekends without her. She talks about his grandmother Elsie's death and how that put him over the edge. She speaks about his physical assault on her that prompted her to call the sheriff. She talks about his father's death and how it occurred a day after his grandmother's. She doesn't give them any information about where she is or how she got there.

She goes on and speaks about Jake's crimes that have happened since he ran off from the sheriff the day he killed his father. He's been on the run since, taking on new identities and murdering others. The last place he was known to be was Phoenix, Arizona, and how he could be anywhere in the country.

Eventually, she talks about her daughter. How it's been almost two years since Jake left, running from the law. She doesn't tell them Hannah's name but they show pictures of her and Hannah. Sadie knows she was lucky to be alive and knows that it was God's will for her to survive. She was pregnant when Jake went on the run and she didn't know it. She also tells them about her staying in a battered women's shelter for two months after that day and how she was scared to even leave and go outside. She feared for her life and she will until he is caught.

Toward the end of the interview, she tells the viewers that Jake is an extremely dangerous man and that if anyone is in contact with him they should call the police immediately. He has killed at least six people.

Two days later the 20/20 episode airs on the television. Laura is too busy pouring drinks to watch it. The television in the bar is normally just background noise to her. One of the patrons asks her to change the channel and she grabs the remote and points it to the television without looking to ESPN.

Jake is watching the broadcast from Laura's house. He's quietly watching and sees pictures flash across the screen. One of them is of his daughter. He looks intently as Sadie does the interview. He tries to look in the background and see if he can see anything familiar but doesn't. He gets his laptop out and searches the story and his name.

He finds the story and looks closely at every shot. He pauses on the photos of his ex and his daughter. He sees something in the background that he recognizes. Laura comes home and he shuts the laptop down. He grabs a knife from the drawer while she is getting a beer from the refrigerator and stabs her to death. He takes her purse and gets in his car and starts driving to Seattle. He empties out her wallet and purse of money and throws them out of the window while he's driving down the exit to the interstate.

Jake saw the space needle in the background of one of the photos of his daughter. He doesn't know where they live in Seattle but he's heading there to find them. Sadie has angered him. He doesn't want any children. He plans to find her and his daughter and kill them.

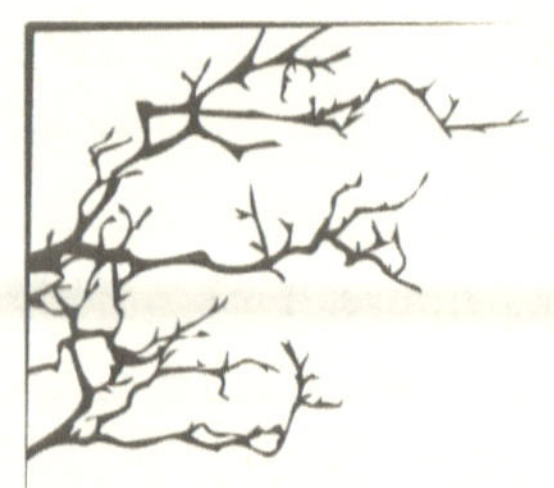

Chapter 14

Many in Jake's hometown saw the 20/20 interview. After it aired, more women came forward to tell their stories about what Jake did to them. Even his old pal Will came forward with stories about Jake. Jake used to brag about his crimes and that he got away with them. Will says he's very slick.

Will tells them about a girl named Stephanie that he met at his house and left with. He noticed that the following Monday she was reported missing. Her body was later found by a fisherman. He tells the sheriff how Jake bragged about raping her and others at his many parties. Will just thought he was making it up until he saw the broadcast.

The sheriff looks into the death of Stephanie Rollins. He asks her mother if they can exhume her body and get a fresh look at her body. Stephanie's mother never believed that her daughter's death was an accident and she tells the sheriff yes. The next day they exhume Stephanie's body. She is taken to the coroner's office for re-examination.

This time the new coroner notes new bruises on her body. She has a mark around her neck showing signs of strangulation. Her hyoid bone is intact. Someone probably strangled her until she was unconscious. They also swab her genital area hoping something will still be there. This is something the original coroner should've done but didn't. They look at the x-rays of her skull and notice how the cracks on the side of her head suggest more than one hit on the head. The new coroner rules her death a homicide.

Now the sheriff can investigate Stephanie's death further. Stephanie is reburied the following day. Her original blood tests were still in the freezer. They have them sent off to the lab for testing. When the results come back her results show that she had little alcohol in her system. She was probably buzzed but not drunk.

Now the Sheriff is more determined to catch Ryan. He shot his brother on purpose which leads to his mother's death. Now they have reason to believe that he killed Stephanie Rollins. He raped multiple girls during his high school years. He's a true psychopath in the Sheriff's eyes.

Sadie, her mother, and Hannah all go about their daily lives. Sadie planned a birthday party for Hannah and her mother helped. A lot of Sadie's and Maude's friends came to the party bringing their children. Even Maude's boyfriend Michael came. He's like a grandfather to Hannah. He loves her dearly. He and Maude have made plans to marry soon. Sadie has already been planning it out.

The birthday party has gone off without a hitch. Hannah is walking now and is enjoying the balloon animals. She makes friends with one of the other toddlers at her party and they play together. When it's time to blow the candle out, she has to have a little help. Hannah helps her blow out her candle. Maude videos it. One of Sadie's friends snaps pictures with the disposable camera Sadie bought.

Sadie gets Hannah to sleep around eight. She's zonked from a busy, fun day. Sadie goes downstairs and talks to her mother and Michael. They are making plans for the wedding. Maude wants a new wedding dress, something simple. She and Sadie make plans to go shopping. She doesn't want a big ceremony and opts for a small venue. Michael also wants a small wedding.

Two weeks later Sadie, her mother, and Hannah are shopping at David's Bridal. Maude picks out a white maxi dress. Sadie buys an emerald-colored flocked tulle low-back dress. They buy a ruffled green and white flower girl dress for Hannah. They buy new heels for the two of them and white dress shoes for Hannah. They leave the store after paying for the items and return home.

Maude grabs the dresses and bags of shoes and carries them into the house while Sadie grabs Hannah from her car seat and carries her inside. She puts Hannah down in the kitchen and grabs a sippy cup to get her some apple juice. She hands the cup to Hannah who walks off toward the kitchen. Maude walks down the stairs and helps Sadie in the kitchen who is now preparing dinner. Hannah watches Teletubbies on the television.

The doorbell rings. Sadie goes to answer it. It's an FBI agent. Sadie allows him to come inside to discuss Jake. Jake is now being investigated by the FBI because his crimes are now in different states across the U.S. Agent Malone tells Sadie and her mother that Jake is now officially a suspect in the death of Stephanie Rollins. The swabs the coroner did on Stephanie's body came back and they matched several rapes that occurred to several of the murder victims. Sadie is aghast.

They want to put an agent on the house in case Jake comes looking for her. He tells her that the interview she did on 20/20 made him snap and that he killed a woman he was living with in Dallas the day it aired. He tells her the woman was Laura Westwood a bartender at a local bar. Jake had lived with her for several months before the show aired.

Sadie feels sick to her stomach. She feels responsible for Laura's death. If she hadn't done the interview she might still be alive. Agent Malone tries to assure her that it wasn't her fault and that Laura would've ended up dead even if the broadcast hadn't happened. He's a ticking time bomb. Maude even tries to reassure her that it wasn't her fault. Sadie runs upstairs and slams her bedroom door shut.

She plops onto the bed and cries. She feels so much guilt. If she would've handled things differently when he had hit her repeatedly, almost killing her this spree of his might not have happened. Then she thinks that it could've been her laying in a casket underground. She thinks that would have been better than feeling the guilt she feels for the deaths he's caused.

Maude runs up the stairs after her. She opens her bedroom door and sees Sadie with a knife to her wrist. She runs and grabs the knife from her daughter and throws it to the ground. She sits on the bed consoling her daughter. The agent heard the commotion and called it in. Sadie will have to be hospitalized for seventy-two hours for trying to commit suicide.

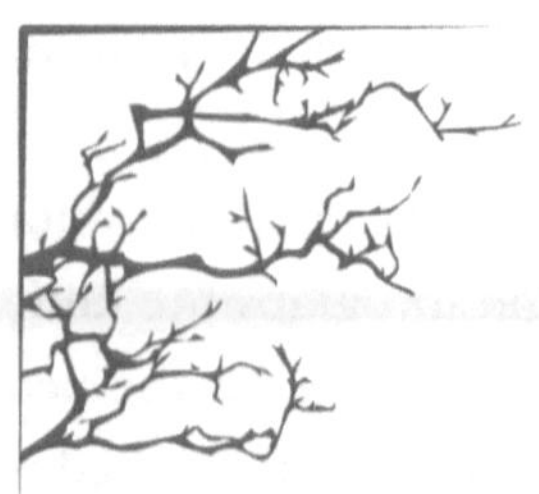

Chapter 15

Sadie is restrained during transport to the hospital. She just lays there on the gurney and looks up at the ceiling of the ambulance. Maude grabs Hannah and follows them in the van. Sadie is taken to the psychiatric ward at the hospital. The doctor gets information from Maude, who is holding Hannah in her lap, about what occurred. She tells Dr. Shandy, a woman, that Agent Malone came by the house and was talking to her and Sadie about her ex-husband Jake. Sadie felt it was her fault for the death of his last known victim. Dr. Shandy asks her why her daughter feels as if it were her fault that the victim was killed. She explains to her about the 20/20 broadcast and how the agent felt it made Jake unstable. The doctor tells Maude that none of Jake's actions is Sadie's fault. She explains to Maude that Sadie will be held for at least seventy-two hours.

Sadie just lays in her hospital bed. She just looks out the window. The nurses come in and give her medicine. It's Zoloft which helps treat depression. Dr. Shandy comes into the room and tries to talk to Sadie. She just lays there, looking out the window and in her own thoughts. She thinks about Hannah and how all of this with Jake could affect her later in life. The next day she is moving around the room some. Dr. Shandy again comes in and tries to talk to her. Sadie asks her what her medicine is. The doctor explains that it's an anti-depressant. Sadie says she isn't depressed.

Sadie goes to group therapy and talks about the things that have happened over the last five years. She tells them about her ex-husband going across the country killing innocent people and not getting caught. She tells them how she feels guilty about it all and that is why she tried to kill herself. The pain inflicted on the victims and their families were almost too much for her to bear.

Others in the group tell her that it wasn't her fault for what her ex did. She tells them that her mother told her the same thing when she took the knife from her. She says that it's difficult for her because she feels like the only survivor in his trail of death and destruction. Dr. Shandy tells her she more than likely has a form of survivor's guilt. She was also a victim of Jake's.

Maude and Michael take care of Hannah while Sadie is in the hospital. Michael came over that night after she got home from the hospital. He's been staying with her for the past three days. Sadie has to sign an agreement before she leaves the hospital. The agreement is that she will not harm herself and if she feels suicidal she will contact someone who can help. Maude, Michael, and Hannah are at the hospital to pick her up.

Jake is in Denver, Colorado. His car broke down. He leaves it on the side of the road and walks into the city. He makes his way to one of the parking garages and looks at the cars. He finds an older model F-150 truck that he breaks into and hotwires. He leaves the garage in the truck and heads out toward the interstate. He makes it to Fort Collins, Colorado, and stops at an exit to get fuel.

He has a long trip ahead of him. He drives until he gets sleepy and stops at a rest area and parks. He sleeps in the truck for a few hours. When the sun starts rising, he leaves the rest area and drives toward his destination. He makes it to Boise, Idaho before he gets a motel for the night. He is still using Charlie's identification.

The FBI has Charlie Holman's name and identification flagged. If it is used, they will get a notification. That's what happens when Jake rents the motel. He pays for the night and gets in the truck and leaves. He saw the look on the motel clerk's face when he saw him. He knew that the clerk knew who he was. Jake was furious. The clerk phones the FBI after Jake leaves.

Jake pulled around to the back of the motel office. He enters through the back door and goes to the office. He pulls his .45 pistol out and shoots the clerk dead. He runs out the back, gets in his truck, and leaves. The FBI office hadn't answered when the clerk called and someone picked up after the shot happened. No one was on the other end of the phone. They hang it up and dial the number back, but it's a busy signal. They run a trace on the number and find that it's to a motel in Fort Collins, Colorado. They notify the local police there to check it out.

The local police arrive at the motel and find the clerk shot dead. They look at the surveillance video and see a man come in shortly before and pay for a room. They show the video to the FBI agent and they believe that it is Jake in the video. They see him drive away from the office. They look through the registration book and see Charlie Holman's name. He's supposed to be in room 102. They go to the room and it is empty. Nobody has been in the room.

Jake is heading northwest. He finds a spot to park near Laramie, Wyoming. He's at a campground in the national forest. He wakes up and drives out of the campground and back onto the interstate. He stops in Laramie and finds a new vehicle to steal. He leaves the truck behind and takes off in the Jeep Cherokee he just stole.

He drives all day after fueling up the Cherokee until he gets to Ogden, Utah. He stops for the night, parking under a bridge near the Willard Bay Reservoir. The FBI has an all-points bulletin out on the truck that Jake stole and on him. They suspect he's heading north toward Seattle. They know he saw the broadcast and that it's possible he found out where Sadie is. Jake sleeps for a few hours under the bridge before seeing a house nearby. He walks up to the house and breaks into the backdoor. He has his pistol on him and he uses it to hit the male occupant over the head knocking him down to the floor. He then stabs him to death. The female occupant screams and Jake runs after her. He stabs her in the leg. She starts crawling, trying to get away from him. He stabs her repeatedly in the back and head.

He hears crying coming from the other bedroom and walks in. A three-year-old little girl is crying. He stabs her to death and places her in her bed. He puts her hands over her chest. He goes to the next bedroom. There's a ten-month-old baby boy asleep in his crib. He stabs him through the heart. He looks through the rest of the house. There's no one else there. He goes and showers. Afterward, he goes to the closet and finds clothes from the male occupant, and finds an outfit. He puts it on.

He goes outside to the back of the house and finds a gas can. It is full of gasoline. He takes it inside and pours gasoline all over the house. When he's done he rummages through the house looking for cash. He cleans out their wallets. He grabs the keys to their car out front and heads toward the front door. He opens the door and lights a match. He sticks the match to the line of gasoline and watches as fire engulfs the house. He runs to the car and gets in. He drives off, looking in the rearview as the house burns.

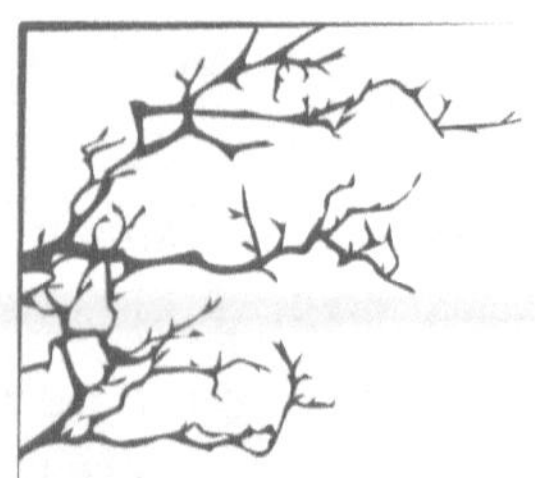

Chapter 16

The house burns for thirty minutes before firefighters arrive. Someone from the road saw the fire and called it in. There were no neighbors around for miles. When the firefighters arrive, the house is almost in ashes. They get the fire out and do a walkthrough. They find bodies in the remains of the house. The fire inspector also walks through and immediately suspects arson. The bodies are put in body bags and taken to the morgue.

When the firefighters saw the bodies of the two young children they got upset. No professional likes to lose a child. They don't like to lose anyone. Children are harder to deal with. They felt guilt over getting there too late. Maybe if there had been advance notice they could've saved the children. The fire inspector also wondered why the adults didn't get out of the house. He suspected it was possibly a murder/arson case. The detectives agreed.

When the coroner checked the remains of the victims, she saw wounds from stabbing. Even the two small children were stabbed to death. None of the victims had smoke or soot in their lungs. She determined that the members of the Mangold household were murdered before the housefire. It didn't help anyone on the case any. They felt even worse and upset that someone could be that cold and kill young children.

The detectives found a truck parked down the road from the house. They run the license and find that it was stolen in Laramie, Wyoming. They forensically check out the truck and find fingerprints all over it. They run the prints through AFIS and get a hit. Jake Morris. The detectives let the FBI know that there was a truck found near a home where a family was murdered. They suspect that it was Jake who had killed them.

They realize one of the family vehicles is gone and put an APB or all points bulletin out on the car. Jake stops in Boise, Idaho, and gets rid of the car. He grabs a gas can from the trunk and sets it on fire. He walks away and finds a vehicle in a car lot. He breaks into it and hot wires it and takes off. It's a vehicle that was in the back waiting for repairs. He drives it until it breaks down near the town of Caldwell, Idaho. He finds another vehicle and drives off into the night.

He has arrived in Seattle, Washington. He pulls into the Seattle Public Library parking lot. He lets the back of his seat down and closes his eyes. He needs a small nap. If someone comes knocking on his window he will explain to them that his wife is inside the library browsing. No one ever knocks on his window. He sleeps for two hours.

When he awakes, he goes inside the library. He uses one of the computers and puts in Sadie's name. He finds her address. He goes outside the library to the payphone and looks through the phone book. He finds her name listed and calls her number. She answers. He hangs up.

Sadie calls Agent Malone and tells him that she had just gotten a hang-up call. She thought it was probably nothing but he told her to let him know if anything out of the ordinary happens. He suspected that Jake was heading to Seattle. He wants to keep Sadie, Hannah, and Maude safe. He runs the number and it shows the call came from the public library. He drives over to Sadie's.

He has the family pack up. He's going to put them in a hotel for the night. They leave their vehicles and two agents stay behind at the house. Jake is making his way through the traffic. He's written down directions to the address listed on the computer. It takes him an hour to get to the address. He drives by and looks at the house. It has a high fence. He leaves and finds a place to park for the night.

He walks to a bar nearby. He starts drinking and dancing with a girl named Sarah. They start making out on the dance floor. They leave together. He drives her to her apartment. They continue making out and have intercourse. He tells her that he just arrived in Seattle and needs a place to stay. She offers for him to stay with her. He accepts.

He drives by Sadie's home almost every day. He never sees her outside. He and Sarah get drunk most nights and party till morning. He isn't working and she works the streets at night. There are times when he goes out with her. When she gets finished with a John he waits outside the room until she leaves and goes in. He usually robs them of their money, threatening to be a cop and threatening to arrest them if they don't give him their money. It's a ruse he and Sarah have been doing for months.

One night the ruse goes too far. Jake is in the room threatening a John and the man charges after him. He pulls his knife out of his pants and stabs the man in the chest as he hurled toward him. The man falls to the ground. He goes through all of his personal items and steals his money, jewelry, and shoes. Sarah doesn't know that Jake killed the man.

Another night the same thing happened. This time Jake stabbed the man under the chin. He stops threatening most of them and starts killing them after Sarah leaves. The Seattle police have been looking for the murderer for months. Jake has raked in over a hundred thousand dollars from the men he kills. Sarah doesn't know that he has been stashing it or that he's been killing anyone.

She is cleaning the apartment one day and finds the money. She asks Jake about it and he tells her it's none of her business. She gets upset and they start arguing. He gets mad and punches her hard. She falls back and hits her head on the coffee table. He grabs a trash bag from under the sink. He realizes she's still alive and puts it over her face and smothers her to death. He then grabs all the money and stuffs it into the trash bag. He leaves the apartment.

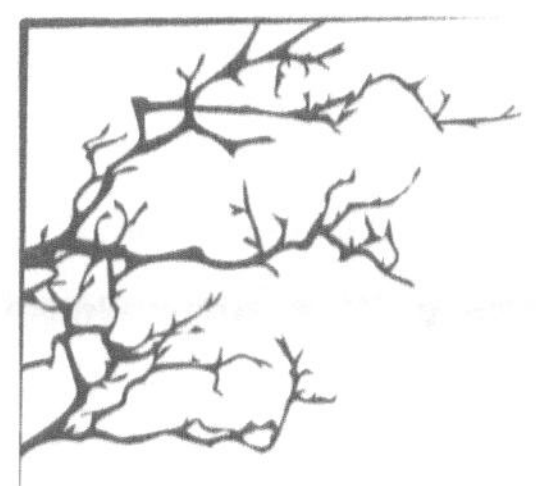

Chapter 17

It's Maude's wedding day. Sadie rented a small church building for the wedding. She had bought green and purple rose bouquets to fill the arch. Sadie, Maude, and Hannah all get in their dresses to walk down the aisle. Michael is standing under the arch as they make their way down the aisle. Friends from Michael's and Sadie's work are there to cheer the couple on. Maude has a few friends there that she plays bridge with. The wedding goes off without a hitch.

Maude and Michael have honeymoon plans in Honolulu, Hawaii. They leave shortly after the reception. Sadie and Hannah get in the car and drive home. Before pulling into her driveway she notices a car parked nearby. She pushes in her code to the gate and it opens. She drives through and the gate closes. She stops and watches as it closes. She opens the garage with the automatic garage opener and drives in. She closes the garage before she gets out of the car.

She gets Hannah out of the car and goes inside. She calls Agent Malone and tells him about the car parked nearby. He sends an agent to drive by the house. They don't find any car parked. They assume that it must have been someone visiting a neighbor. Agent Malone calls Sadie back and tells her.

Sadie gets Hannah's dress off and puts her in the tub. She finishes washing her up and gets her out. She puts pajama's on Hannah and gets her ready for bed. She reads her Green Eggs and Ham before tucking her into her toddler bed. She turns on the lava lamp before turning her light off and closing her door. She walks downstairs.

She is sitting on the sofa watching television. She sees the 20/20 broadcast airing again that she did. They have also added to it.

Other victims are speaking out about what Jake did to them in high school. She sees his old friend Will on the television talking about him bragging about killing a girl named Stephanie. Sadie realizes she wasn't his only surviving victim. Now she fears that Jake will go after those speaking out.

Jake has left Seattle. He is heading back to his hometown Miles City, Montana. He saw the broadcast and now has vengeance in his head. Sadie and his daughter can wait. He drives all night. He drives to his former farmhouse. He knows where the bunker is. He gets inside the bunker and turns on the lights. There is food there. He puts the bag of money in a footlocker. He looks through the closet and finds black clothing and a black balaclava mask. When it's nightfall, he leaves the bunker and walks through the woods toward his friend Will's house. He breaks in and shoots him while he's sleeping. He also shoots the woman in the bed with Will.

He leaves the house. He goes back to the bunker. He strips his clothes off and sits on the cot. He smacks his head with his hands and yells out. He showers and heads to bed. Tomorrow he will find the others.

He dresses in his black outfit and balaclava. He runs through the woods. He has his father's old sniper rifle on his back. He has his military knife in its sash on his side. He has his pistol in its holster on his opposite side. He has his face covered in black makeup.

He finds his next target. He aims through the scope of his rifle into the home of Camille. He sees her at the kitchen sink washing dishes. He aims with precision and shoots her through the head. He sees her husband and shoots him dead. He gets up from his spot and runs off.

He is now outside the home of the sheriff. He looks through his scope, waiting for a shot. Sheriff Grilles is in his recliner watching television. Jake aims his gun at the sheriff's head and squeezes the trigger. He hits the sheriff in his head. Killing him instantly. He sees his wife running up to the body and Jake shoots her. She falls to the floor. He gets up and runs back to his bunker.

He parked the car nearby and covered it with brush. He grabs things from the bunker days later and loads the car. He has his rifle, his knife, his pistol, the money, extra clothes, and ammunition loaded in the car. He waits a few more days for the heat to die down before he takes off.

He's heading back to Seattle. He has to finish Sadie and his daughter. He doesn't want his bloodline going any further than him. The FBI now knows he was in his hometown. They ran ballistics from the six victims and have matched the pistol to the murder of James Waters and his father's rifle, the one that killed his brother Tate fifteen years prior.

They know that Jake is responsible for the deaths of Will and his girlfriend, Sheriff Grilles, and his wife, and Camille Bryan and her husband. He has now killed over a dozen people. Agent Malone calls Sadie and tells her that Jake is cleaning house. He suspects that she will be his next target. She agrees to let agents stay at her house. She fixes up her mother's old room as a guest room. Her mother moved out before her wedding to Michael.

Agent Sadler is assigned to stay at the house. Agent Sadler is a young agent. He's been at the bureau for over five years now. He's almost thirty years old. Sadie is slightly uncomfortable around Agent Sadler. It could be because of his age and occupation. He comes to the house dressed in plain clothes and carrying a suitcase. Sadie sets him up in the guest room. He unpacks his suitcase and puts his clothes in the drawers. He keeps his pistol concealed under his clothes. Sadie knows it's there and she tries to ignore it.

Agent Sadler checks the house periodically during the night. He doesn't sleep at night. He closes all of the blinds when the sun starts to set. He usually sits with the television on mute listening to the noises from outside. He does a walk-through of the house every hour. He checks on both Sadie and Hannah while they sleep.

Jake has made it back to Seattle. He looks at the map of the area near Sadie's house. He's trying to figure out a way to get to her and his daughter. He looks for tall buildings near her home. He finds one. He needs a new identification. They always ask for ID when paying for a hotel room.

He buys prosthetic makeup and facial hair at one of the shops nearby. He pickpockets a wallet from one of the men shopping at the store. He pays for his items and leaves. He goes and parks. He uses the makeup and facial hair to make himself look different. He then finds a white-painted wall to stand in front of and takes a picture of himself. He takes apart the driver's license from the wallet he stole. He cuts out the picture he took and replaces the one on the driver's license with it. He then tapes it up with packing tape.

He drives to the hotel and gives them his driver's license. They register him under his assumed name, David Reynolds. He carries his bags upstairs to the elevator. He asked for a room on the top floor. He goes up the elevator to the top floor. He gets out of the elevator and walks to his room. He opens the door and walks in, shutting the door behind him. He opens his bag and gets out the rifle. He places it on the table. He looks out the window with his binoculars. He's looking for Sadie's house.

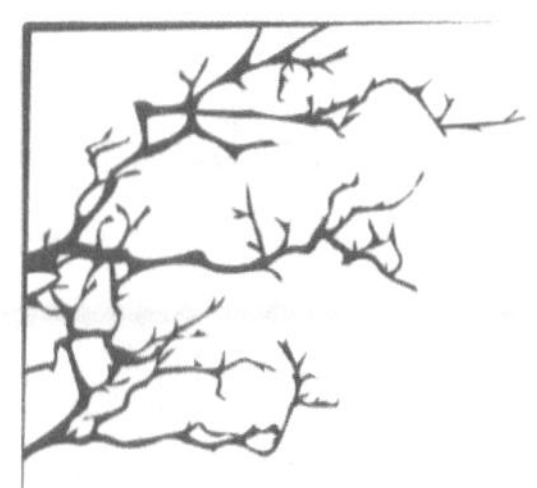

Chapter 18

Maude and Michael have returned from their honeymoon. Maude comes and visits Sadie and Hannah. She shows them pictures from the honeymoon. Sadie is happy for her mother. Micheal is a nice guy and she deserves someone like him. They all go out to dinner that night.

Hannah will soon be two years old. Sadie spends her days at work while Maude watches Hannah. Agent Malone insists that Maude come to the house and watch Hannah so they can protect them.

Jake paid a month on the room. He uses room service to get dinner. He pays them cash. He doesn't leave the room during his stay. He stands at the window looking through his binoculars and rifle scope. He sees a man standing in Sadie's living room at the window. He never sees her or his daughter.

Agent Sadler walks around the perimeter of the house. Jake watches as the agent walks around the yard. He wonders what the man is doing. He watches him closely as he goes inside, locks the door, and pulls the blinds. He puts the scope down on the table.

Jake watches the house as the sun is coming up. He can see the lights in the house come on. He saw the light from the television all night. He finds the habits of his ex-wife and her man friend odd. The blinds open and he sees Sadie standing by the window. He sees the man sitting on the sofa. He watches as the man gets up off the sofa and walks to her. The blinds close again.

Sadie is talking to Agent Sadler about the blinds. They never told her how the six in her hometown died by Jake. The agent lets it slip. He tells her that Jake shot them with a high-powered rifle from a long distance. Sadie gets upset and runs to her room. Now she understands why the agent keeps the blinds closed. She's scared to leave her house now. She's also scared to stay there. She doesn't know what to do. She cries herself back to sleep and misses work.

Maude comes over at her usual time to babysit Hannah. She realizes that Sadie is still there and is in her room. The agent tells her what happened. Maude gets upset because they should've told them earlier what happened to the last six victims. She makes a call to Agent Malone telling him her frustration.

Maude gets Hannah up and feeds her breakfast. Agent Sadler goes upstairs to the bedroom to sleep. Sadie is still in her room sleeping. She wakes up screaming. Agent Sadler jumps out of bed with his pistol in his hand looking around. Maude has Hannah in her arms as she's running up the stairs. They both enter Sadie's room. Sadie is crying and upset. Agent Sadler holsters his pistol. Sadie had a bad dream.

Hannah puts her hand on her mother's shoulder. Sadie hugs and kisses her. She wraps her arms around Hannah and holds her tightly. Maude rubs Sadie's back trying to calm her down. She's upset from the dream. She's scared Jake is going to kill her and Hannah.

Sadie postpones Hannah's birthday party. She's scared out of her skull about what could happen. They celebrate with a cake and presents with Maude and Michael in attendance. She has heard the agent talking to Agent Malone and she knows that there are many more victims than she knows about. She overheard him talking on the phone about a house fire where Jake had killed all four family members, two of them small children. She's freaked out.

Jake watches the house intently. His time for the month is almost up. He puts his makeup back on, goes to the lobby, and pays for another month on the room. He continues watching the house. He uses his scope more than his binoculars. He can see everything clearer with the scope.

Agent Sadler continues his routine. Agent Malone has been doing searches trying to find where Jake is hiding out. They run his name and image through their databases hoping to get a hit. So far, they've had no luck. He wants to catch him before he kills anyone else.

Jake is tired of sitting in his room and watching. He puts his rifle in his bag and pushes it under his bed. He goes down the elevator to the lobby with his face disguised and walks to his car. He drives to the backside of Sadie's house and looks around. He sees a small trail. He gets out of the car and walks the trail to see where it ends. It ends at the fence on the back of the property next door.

He drives back to his hotel. He gets to his room and starts looking at the house next door. He sees the occupants packing suitcases and putting them by the door. He watches as they leave the house the following morning on the airport shuttle. He suspects they will be gone for at least a few days. He packs up his belongings and leaves his room. He gets to the lobby and walks out the door. He gets in his car and drives to the back of the house next door.

He goes up the trail and climbs over the fence. He breaks into the house. He goes inside and walks up to the second floor. He sees a door to the attic. He pulls it down and walks up the steps. He looks around. He sees wall louvers at each end of the attic. He looks out through the cracks and sees his ex's house. He goes back downstairs and to the garage.

He grabs some chemicals from under the kitchen sink. He mixes them. He knows that if he lets them brew that they'll eventually blow up the house. He leaves the house and climbs back over the fence. He goes back to his hotel and waits for the house to explode. After two hours of waiting, he hears a loud boom. He put a silencer on his rifle. He has cut open a small hole with his glass cutter in the window for his barrel to go through.

Sadie and Agent Sadler also hear the boom and run out the back door. He has his rifle aimed at Sadie's head. He squeezes the trigger.

Before the bullet reaches its target Sadie moves. She is grazed in the head and falls to the ground. Agent Sadler looks around after dropping to the ground. He crawls over to Sadie who is holding her head. Sadler gets his phone out and calls 911 and Agent Malone.

Jake is waiting for them to get up off the ground. He knows the shot didn't kill Sadie. He can see her moving on the ground below. Agent Sadler is covering her with his body. Hannah is walking toward the door. Agent Sadler gets up off of Sadie and rushes to Hannah. Jake shoots him in the back and he falls on top of Hannah. Sadie crawls to her daughter. Jake shoots in front of her while she is crawling. She finally makes it into the door and closes the blinds.

He missed her. Agent Malone makes it to the house within five minutes. The ambulance arrives shortly after. Firetrucks and police arrive a moment later and work on the fire from the house next door. Jake watches from his hand-held scope as it all unfolds. The paramedics put Agent Sadler on the gurney and rush him to the hospital. Sadie gets patched up from the graze on her head and Agent Malone packs her and Hannah into his car and drives off with them.

The police leave the scene after FBI investigators show up to process the scene. They look to see where the shots could have come from. Jake had tried to shoot Hannah but shot the agent instead. He was furious. He gathers his belongings and leaves the hotel. He drives to the hospital. He suspects that's where they took Sadie. He watches the entranceway. He never sees her.

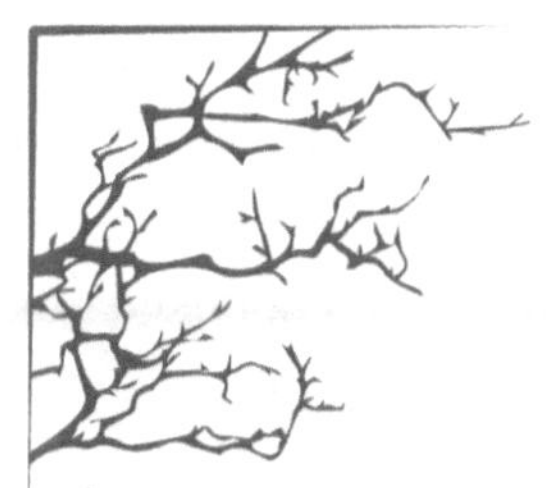

Chapter 19

The investigators have determined that the shot came from the hotel. They go and look for a room where the shot could've come from and was occupied. They find the room where Jake was staying. They see the hole cut out in the window. They process the room. They ask for the person's name that stayed in the room. The hotel manager gladly gives it to the FBI. They also want security footage.

Agent Malone has taken Sadie and Hannah to the helipad. They board a helicopter and fly to Bend, Oregon. The FBI has a safe house in the area and put Sadie and Hannah up there. They feel that they will be safe there. Agent Malone stays with them. He has the local doctor check out both of them and he puts butterfly closures on Sadie's head wound.

Agent Malone checks on the status of Agent Sadler. He's still in surgery. No other word yet on how he's doing. He's visibly upset because his agent got shot. Sadie is scared to death. The FBI has determined that the shot that hit Agent Sadler was meant for Hannah. They tell Agent Malone.

Agent Malone is getting irritated because Jake hasn't been caught yet. He shot an agent with the FBI. He hopes Agent Sadler will be alright. He's too young to die and has his entire life ahead of him. Sadie sits in the corner of the bedroom holding Hannah tight. Hannah just sits there with her mother. She is too young to understand what is going on but she is visibly scared about what happened. She soon falls asleep in Sadie's arms.

Jake hits the steering wheel in frustration and anger as he leaves the hospital parking lot. He has lost his targets. He drives, leaves Seattle, and heads east. He arrives in Spokane a little over four hours later. He is parked at the airport watching people go by. He sees a man that is similar to him in size and gets out of his car, grabs his small bag, and follows him. When the man isn't paying attention he pickpockets his wallet. Jake goes to the airport bathroom. He opens the wallet and gets out the license. He uses the same photo as before and inserts it in place of the man's photo and tapes up the new driver's license.

He grabs the longer beard out of his bag and glues it to his face. He leaves the restroom and goes to the ticket counter. He purchases a ticket to New York City. The flight is leaving in half an hour so he waits for time to board. He boards the Boeing 747 and puts his small bag in the carry-on and sits in his seat. His flight takes off and he's on his way to the Big Apple.

Agent Sadler was shot in his lower left-back. The bullet mutilated his kidney and lodged in his hip bone. The surgeons had to remove his left kidney and the bullet that was lodged in his hip. They take the bullet and put it in a plastic container so it can be analyzed. He is now in recovery.

Agent Malone is at the hospital with Agent Sadler. He had another agent sitting with Sadie and Hannah at the safehouse and flew back. He gets word that Jake has possibly left the state. They don't know where he's gone but have found footage of him at the airport in Spokane. Agent Sadler awakens and looks around his room and sees Agent Malone sitting in the chair. Agent Malone gets up and talks to him, telling him that he's going to be alright. Agent Sadler asks about Sadie and Hannah. He wants to know that they are alright. Agent Malone assures him that they are safe. He falls back asleep.

Maude and Michael get notified of what happened at Sadie's home. They are also told that the two are now in a safe place. Maude demands to see her daughter and granddaughter. The FBI agent tells her that right now she can't. She gets upset and slams the door in the agent's face. She calls Agent Malone and asks him. He explains to Maude that

Sadie and Hannah are at an undisclosed location in a safe house with an agent on them. He tells her that she'll get to see them soon. They need to locate Jake.

Jake lands in New York hours later. He gets off the plane and hails a taxi. He is going to a motel for the night. He still has his disguise on and when he checks in he uses the alias he got when he was in Spokane. He walks around the city during the day looking at and watching all of the people. He'll be lost in a haven of other bodies. He finally feels free.

The FBI goes to the Spokane airport and asks the ticket counter if they remember seeing the man in the picture. They claim he could have a beard or other type of facial hair. The man in the picture is Jake, a fugitive for almost three years who has evaded capture. The ticket saleswoman says he looks familiar and they ask to see security footage. They find him at the ticket stand in the video. They ask where he purchased a ticket to and they look up ticket sales from the timestamp.

Jake is now Jared Morrison and in New York City. The FBI puts out an APB on his new alias and notify the New York City Police. They tell the New York police that Jake a.k.a. Jared Morrison is a very dangerous individual. When they locate the actual Jared Morrison they ask him if he has seen or knows Jake Morris. Jared doesn't know the name or the person. Jared realized that his wallet was missing when he was at the airport. He told the FBI that someone had to have taken it between the parking garage and the ticket counter because when he went to get his ticket the wallet was gone and he had just put it in his pocket when he left the car. Now the FBI knows how Jake got a new identity.

It's been a week and Agent Sadler is getting released from the hospital. Sadie and Hannah return home from the safehouse. Sadie decides to move from her home of three years for a fresh start. Sadie visited Agent Sadler at the hospital and thanked him for saving Hannah's life.

Sadie and Hannah's belongings are loaded up in the moving truck. She has bought a new house on the other side of Seattle. She'll be closer to her mother and step-father. There aren't any tall buildings nearby that Jake can hide at and try to shoot them from. She also makes sure that her name can't be found and uses her mother's name for all of her utilities.

Agent Malone has a new agent assigned to Sadie and Hannah while Agent Sadler recovers. Agent Flannery is an older agent. He's different than Sadler. He doesn't talk much. He just observes. He stays up all night just like Sadler did but only sleeps a few hours during the day. Sadie feels even more uncomfortable with him around.

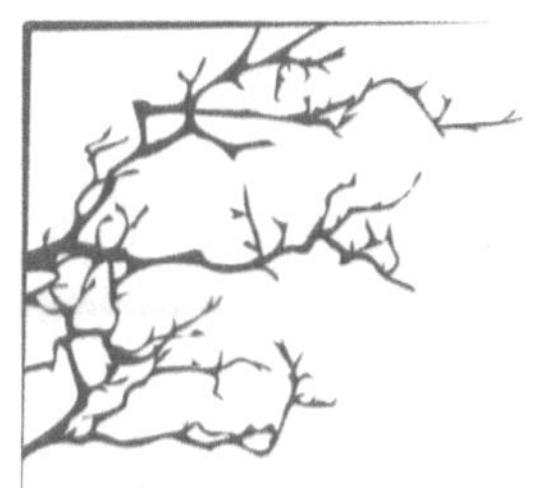

Chapter 20

It's been three months since Jake went to New York. He's made new friends and has started doing drugs again. He's even dating a young woman, Ellie Meadows. He has a minimum wage job and has a small apartment. The FBI is continually running his aliases and name through their system trying to locate him. They find plenty of Jake Morris' but they're only looking for a certain one. They haven't had any hits on Jared's name in months. They believe he's not using that alias anymore.

Sadie spends time with Agent Sadler. She goes to his physical therapy sessions and roots him on. She feels indebted to him for saving Hannah's life. After the physical therapy she takes him out for lunch and they talk. They have gotten to know each other personally.

Agent Nicholas Sadler is originally from Green Bay, Wisconsin. His parents are both alive and still married. He'll be thirty-three in December. He's never been married and went to Quantico for training when he was twenty-three. After graduating high school at the age of seventeen, he went to college and got his bachelor's degree in Criminal Justice. He has always wanted to be an FBI agent.

This assignment was the first one he'd been shot during. He asked to be assigned to Sadie and Hannah. He wanted to protect them. He knew that Sadie had been a victim of Jake's for years and he felt compelled to help. He knows Jake and has studied the case files for years. He and Agent Malone both know Jake from studying his crimes and actions. When Jake shot and killed the Sheriff, it surprised them. He never thought that Jake would kill the sheriff of his hometown. He had no reason to.

They also know that Jake won't stop coming for Sadie and his daughter. They know he will kill his own daughter because he killed the two small Mangold children in Utah. They know he's a genuine psychopath. He has no empathy. They also know that to stop him, they'll have to kill him.

Jake is living with Ellie in New York. Ellie is a dancer at the Art Institute. Jake works as a taxi cab driver. He has a new alias, Faroq Abdillah. He killed Faroq and threw his body in the Hudson River. His body hasn't been found. Faroq isn't the only person Jake has killed. There have been others but the crimes remain unsolved.

Ellie doesn't know that Jake is a murderer. They use drugs when they aren't working or dancing. One night Ellie takes too much heroin and overdoses. Jake calls an ambulance and leaves their loft. Ellie is taken to the hospital and her stomach is pumped. She's unconscious for weeks but makes it. When she is released from the hospital she checks herself into rehab. Jake hasn't been back to the loft.

Jake has moved on with a new woman, Kristin Davies. Kristin was someone he had met while living with Ellie. He and Kristin had been secretly dating for a month. He moved in with her after he left the loft. He had a vasectomy done shortly after he arrived in New York. He used his bag of cash to get it done. He and Kristen do their usual everyday and weekend.

Kristin works as a hairstylist at a local beauty shop. Two months later she announces to Jake that she's pregnant. He knows the baby isn't his and he gets angry with her. He smacks her and asks her who she has been cheating with. When she refuses to answer and denies his allegation he strangles her. He leaves her on the floor of the apartment and leaves after grabbing his things.

Jake is at work driving his taxi around the city. He makes small talk with most of his passengers while driving them to their destinations. One night he picks up a rich, young woman named Summer Martin.

She is from the prominent Martin family of New York who has made billions with their networking business.

He drives to a secluded part of town. Summer tried to escape when he didn't take an exit he was supposed to and he reached back and knocked her unconscious. He hit her with a small bat he had in the front seat with him. When he gets to the spot he wants to be, he grabs her out of the back of the taxi. She is beginning to regain consciousness. He throws her onto the trunk of the taxi and holds her down while he rapes her from behind. He uses her scarf to strangle her. He leaves her body on the ground, in the tall grass several feet away from where he was parked.

He grabs her small handbag from the backseat and rummages through it, taking her money before throwing it on the ground next to her. He gets in the taxi and drives back to the city. He picks up a new customer and drops them off at their destination. For the rest of the night, he drops the customers off at their destinations.

Kristin and Summer are both discovered and both scenes processed. Summer's father, James Martin has put out a reward for any information regarding his daughter's death. When they run the fingerprints and forensics everything comes back to Jake Morris. His fingerprints were found in Kristin's apartment and on her neck. Semen from Summer's rape kit was that of Jake's. The New York police now have a suspect. They now need to find him.

They know that Jake has been on the run for over three years. They notify the FBI of their findings. Jake's face is now being plastered across billboards in New York City. The NYPD and the FBI are determined to capture him. Jake sees this and leaves the city, driving his taxi. He abandons the taxi when he gets to New Jersey and steals a truck. He is heading south down the eastern seaboard.

Nick and Sadie have been spending more time together. Nick has gotten back to his normal self and his physical therapy has ended. He has taken over being the agent in charge of her but this time it's different. He doesn't act like a robot. He acts like a father to Hannah and a husband to Sadie. He and Sadie have fallen in love over the past six months. Sadie is taking it slow as is Nick. It's usually frowned upon in the FBI to date the person you are guarding.

Agent Malone doesn't see a problem with Nick and Sadie dating. He does tell Nick to be careful. Maude has the same advice for Sadie even though she is happy Sadie has found someone. Hannah will be three soon and this year, Sadie is set on holding a birthday bash for her. She didn't have one the year before. She invites members of the FBI to attend. Agent Malone is even in attendance.

Jake has made it to Miami, Florida. His taxi was located and processed by the New Jersey state police. They found Jake's fingerprints all over it. They even found the small bat he kept in the front seat. They process the bat and find blood on it from not only Summer Martin but others. Now they're scared he's killed others that they don't know about.

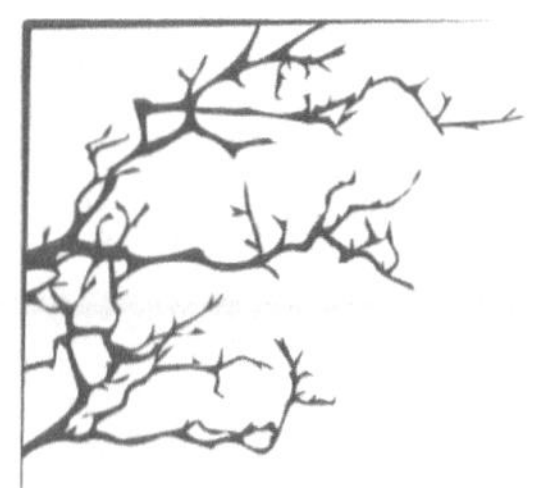

Chapter 21

Two years have passed since Jake arrived in Miami. He now goes by the name Jason Laymon. He's married to Trish. He has settled down. He has a job at a local fishery. He has grown out his beard and hair. Trish is an older woman, nearly forty, and has a grown daughter. Her daughter Shayla is in college in New Hampshire.

Sadie and Nick were married a year earlier. They left Seattle and moved to his hometown of Green Bay, Wisconsin. Hannah has started kindergarten. Maude and Michael still live in Seattle, Washington. Maude and Michael fly frequently to see Sadie and her family. Nick thinks he can keep Sadie and Hannah safe. Sadie changed her last name to her married name and Nick adopted Hannah. Sadie is also pregnant with their first child together. She is due in July.

Social media has taken off. Myspace and Facebook are now competing. Jake made a Myspace account and when Facebook started getting more recognition, he and his wife both made profiles. Sadie and Nick don't use social media. He still works for the FBI and knows that the bureau watches for threats on social media.

Jake uploaded a selfie of himself and his wife and used it as his profile picture on Facebook. The FBI has been trying to locate him for ten years now. They continually check for facial recognition. He's been quiet for four years now. They have no idea where he went.

Sadie and Nick's son Jonah is now four years old. Hannah is nine. Maude and Michael have moved to Green Bay to be closer to the grandchildren. They are both retired. Nick is no longer in the field but has a desk job in the FBI field office. Agent Malone is still a supervisor with the FBI.

Cell phones are also more popular. Sadie and Nick both have one. They call each other regularly to check in with one another. Jake and his wife Trish also have cell phones. Jake thinks the FBI has given up on finding him. He's not worried anymore. He believes he has escaped their clutches for good. He does think about Sadie and Hannah often. He gets upset when he thinks about how close he came to ending them and wasn't able to.

Trish's daughter Shayla is now married. One of her favorite past times is watching police procedural television shows. CSI: NY is one of the more popular shows that she watches. She also loves watching Law & Order: SVU. One night she is watching an airing of 20/20. She gets hooked on it. She looks online and finds a streaming service that has the show on it. She binge watches it for weeks. It takes almost a month of binge-watching for the 20/20 episode about serial killer Jake Morris. He looks familiar to her.

Her husband, Shane also watches the show with her. He asks her if that is her step-father when he sees the photos of Jake Morris on the television screen. Shayla gasps in shock. She writes down the number shown on the screen and dials it from her cell phone. She tells the woman who answers that she knows Jake Morris. The woman on the other end of the phone puts Shayla on hold.

Her call is transferred to Agent Malone. Shayla tells him that she believes that Jake Morris is her step-father Jason Laymon who is married to her mother and lives in Miami, Florida. Agent Malone asks her why she thinks it's the same man and she tells him about a tattoo on Jason's arm that looks exactly like the one in the picture of Jake Morris. He takes her information and tells her not to say anything to anyone, not even her mother. He explains to her that if Jake is Jason and her mother were to find out, she'd be in mortal danger.

Agent Malone runs to his office and asks two of his agents to look up Jason Laymon on social media. They find fifty different Jason Laymon's on Facebook. Then he tells the agents to find the one that lives in Miami, Florida. There is one hit. Agent Malone sits down at the computer and looks through the profile. He sees pictures of the man known as Jason Laymon. They run the photos through facial recognition with Jake Morris's photo and get a match.

They run Jason Laymon's name and find an address and other information on him. Agent Malone and his two other agents board a plane to Miami. They have found their man after almost two decades. When they arrive in Miami, Florida they go to the FBI office in Miami.

Agent Malone and his two agents, Kendrick and Williams, devise a plan to capture Jake Morris a.k.a. Jason Laymon without any casualties. Kendrick and Williams will stay at a home nearby and surveil the Laymon home. They will watch and see when Jake leaves and returns. They plan to surveil for a week and on Friday morning when Jake leaves his home and goes to work they will stop him and arrest him, hopefully without incident.

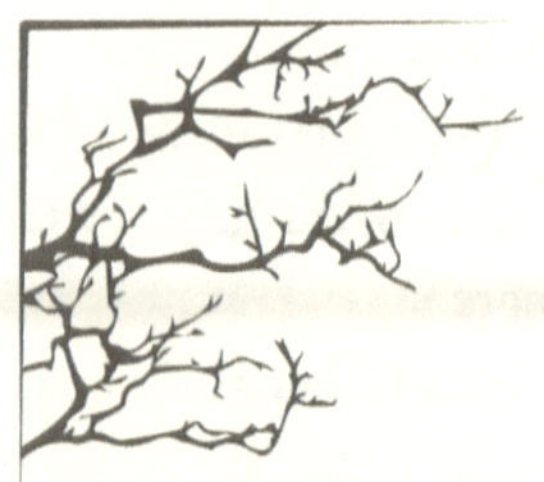

Chapter 22

While Jake and his wife are gone for the day, Kendrick slips over to the Laymon home and installs video cameras and listening devices inside the home. They can do better surveillance on the home and hear any plans that Jake makes that could interfere with their plans to apprehend him. Kendrick gets finished and makes his way out of the home and back over across the street to his rental home.

That evening, Trish Laymon knocks on their door. She has brought them a welcome to the neighborhood gift. Kendrick and Williams claim to be gay men in love with each other. She is talking to them on their porch when Jake arrives home. He comes over and introduces himself. The four of them talk a few minutes more before Trish and Jake leave to go to their house.

Shayla has been googling Jake Morris. She finds that the second 20/20 episode aired about him years ago. She also finds newspaper articles about his crimes. She is mortified at everything she finds. She wants to call her mother but remembers what Agent Malone said to her. Her mother would be in mortal danger if she were to find out and confront Jake.

Agent Williams listens in on the conversations that Jake and Trish have. They know that Trish is planning a trip to New Hampshire to see her daughter in two weeks. They know that Jake is going out on a boat next week to fish and will be gone for months. He tells Agent Malone what they have found out.

Agent Malone gets a swat team together to siege the home of Jake and Trish. They will do it at night while they are asleep. They make plans to do it Thursday morning. They want to bring Jake in alive. He needs to know his actions have consequences. While Trish and Jake are at work on Wednesday, Agent Kendrick makes his way back into the Laymon home. He uses a metal detector to see if there are any firearms in the home. He doesn't find any. He leaves and comes back to his house.

It's three o'clock in the morning. Agent Malone and the swat team go inside the Laymon home. Jake and Trish wake up startled. Trish is scared out of her wits wondering what was going on. Agent Malone walks up to Jake and handcuffs him. He tells Jake that he is under arrest and mirandizes him as they walk down the hallway and out of the house. Trish is freaking out and crying. She grabs a robe and puts it on. She is asking them what is going on.

After Malone puts Jake in the car and the two agents drive off. He goes back inside to talk to Trish. He tells her that the FBI got a call from her daughter Shayla after she watched an episode of 20/20 realizing that her mother was married to the serial killer Jake Morris. Trish gasps in shock. Her Jason has always been good to her. She couldn't believe that he was this Jake Morris person that they believe him to be.

Jake is taken to the FBI field office in Miami. He is fingerprinted and then handcuffed to the table in the interrogation room. He sits there for over an hour waiting. Malone walks into the room with a large group of folders under his arm. He sits the group of folders on the table and sits. He looks at Jake and asks him his name. Jake tells him, Jason Laymon. Malone looks at him and tells him that he knows that isn't his real name. Jake repeats himself.

Malone opens the first folder and pulls out a fingerprint card. He tells Jake that his prints match those of Jake Morris. He acts like he doesn't understand. Malone tells Jake that they have a court order for his DNA. Jake stops talking. He doesn't say anything as Malone continues to ask him questions. After ten minutes, Jake puts his hand up to stop Malone from talking and says "lawyer". Malone grabs the folders and leaves the interrogation room.

Malone calls Nick and tells him they have Jake in custody. Nick tells Sadie and she starts jumping up and down excitedly. She is in awe. They finally have him in custody. This horrible, awful man who has been terrorizing people since he was a teenager. Now she hopes he will get what he deserves.

Agent Malone has his work cut out for him. He has over 20 murders in at least five different states that Jake committed. He killed the sheriff in his hometown along with several others. They have the death penalty there. He killed several in New York City including a prominent family's daughter. He can get life there. He shot an FBI agent and killed others along the way to Seattle, Washington. He killed a family of four in Utah, including two small children under the age of 3. He can get the death penalty there.

The forensic technician goes inside the interrogation room to get a sample of Jake's blood for DNA analysis. This is one of the most guaranteed ways to prove who he is. Fingerprints are also but for definitive indisputable proof, DNA was best. That will make his prosecution airtight.

Trish is at the FBI office talking to Agent Malone. Malone tells her what Jake has done. That his fingerprints match and that they are now running his DNA even though it's on file. She's upset because she doesn't understand how this happened. Agent Malone tells her that a few serial killers have lived normal lives with others for decades before being found out and brought to justice. She tells Malone that she hopes Jake gets the electric chair. She wants nothing more to do with him. She leaves the building.

She returns home and calls her daughter. Shayla apologizes for not letting her know and tells her what the FBI told her. She isn't made at her daughter. She's mad at herself for being duped. She realizes that she could've been killed at any moment by the man she was married to.

Jake is put in a cell until transport can be arranged. Malone talked to the federal prosecutor and asked for his advice. He thinks Jake should be tried in Montana for the murders he committed there. Then Utah, Washington State, New York, Texas, California, and all other states can prosecute Jake for his crimes.

Jake is meeting with his attorney that was called in after he asked for one. He declines to talk to Agent Malone. He insists on talking to Sadie. Malone won't allow it. He then tells Malone that he has nothing else to say.

Malone calls Sadie and tells her that Jake wants to talk to her. He tells her that he is refusing to talk to anyone else. He advises her that it's a bad idea. Sadie tells him she needs to think about it. Sadie talks to Nick about it. Nick tells her that it's up to her. If it were him, he wouldn't let her but it's not his decision. Sadie agrees to try to talk to Jake.

Sadie leaves Hannah and Jonah with her mother. She and Nick catch a plane to Miami. They arrive at the FBI office hours later. Agent Malone has Jake brought back to the interrogation room. Jake's attorney is also there. Sadie watches from the other room as Jake is brought into the room and cuffed to the table. She watches as he sits there in his seat conversing with his attorney. Agent Malone walks in and tells Jake that Sadie will be in shortly to speak with him.

Sadie is nervous. She takes a deep breath and walks into the room. She grabs the empty chair across from Jake and moves it to the wall. She sits and looks at him. She asks him what he wants to talk about. He doesn't speak but looks at her. His blue eyes are cold and empty. His face was expressionless. His body was anchored. Sadie doesn't flinch. She asks him again what he wants to talk to her about. He sits there staring at her. She gets up from the chair and smacks her hand down on the table hard and tells him that there is nothing he can say to her that will change anything. He doesn't move. His attorney winces. She tells him that he is a monster and that hell wouldn't be horrible enough for him and leaves the room.

Jake doesn't move. He just sits there as she walks out the door. Sadie goes back to the room next door and asks Agent Malone what happens next. He tells her that he will be transported back to Montana and then the next state that is prosecuting him and the next. Sadie thinks that's a lot of movement for someone that's been on the run for over ten years. She doesn't like the idea.

Jake starts talking to the mirror in the interrogation room. It's as if he's looking through the two-way mirror and at Sadie. He tells her she's still beautiful but she deserves to die. He then threatens her telling her he will finish her and his daughter and that no prison cell will stop him. He suddenly stops talking. Sadie is upset. Nick puts his arms around her to console her.

Jake is taken back to his cell. He will be transported to Montana in the morning. Agent Malone, Agent Williams, and Agent Kendrick will all be traveling with him. If he tries to escape, they will shoot and kill him.

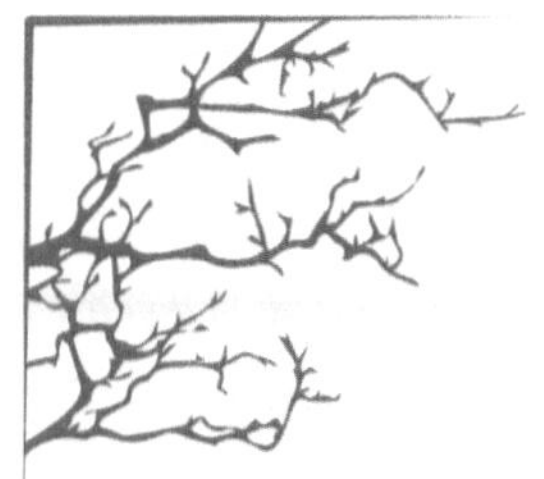

Chapter 23

Jake has been in jail in Montana for over a year. His attorney keeps filing motions, therefore, making the case drag out longer. The prosecutors from New York and Utah have been waiting and watching the case unfold in Montana. Jake wants to make a deal but the prosecution won't allow anything less than the death penalty since he killed the sheriff.

Three months later jurors are selected for the trial at the Yellowstone County Courthouse in Billings, Montana. Miles City, Montana where Jake is from is a small town and wouldn't have impartial jurors. Most of the townspeople know each other. The prosecution asked that the trial be moved to Billings where jurors wouldn't know the defendant. The defense didn't have a problem with it.

Jury selection takes two days. There are five men and seven women on the jury with three alternates. The prosecution hopes that the trial doesn't take longer than a month. It shouldn't. Most of their evidence against the defendant is ballistics.

Jake's lawyer tries to show that someone else had used the gun to shoot the sheriff and his wife. The prosecution tells the jury that not only were the sheriff and his wife murdered that night but four others were also. Two with the same rifle as the sheriff and the other two with a pistol that had been used in other crimes committed by the defendant. The prosecution also tells the jury that three of the victims had spoken out against the defendant in a 20/20 interview.

The sheriff's deputy that was at the scene when Jake punched the sheriff and his father, knocking his father down and killing him also testified. Sadie was there and also told the jury what happened that day when Jake took off twelve years ago. She also tells the jury how Jake knew Will, one of the victims. She even tries to tell them about Jake trying to assassinate her but his attorney objects. The judge overrules. She tells them that Jake had grazed her with a bullet and then aimed at her daughter Hannah trying to kill her. She states that her daughter was two years old at the time and that an FBI agent had shielded Hannah from the bullet, he was wounded.

The defense rested and closing arguments would start tomorrow. It's been three weeks since the trial started. Sadie sits in the courtroom every day watching. She returns to her hotel room with Nick and sleeps. She's exhausted. This will probably be the only hearing she will go to besides the one in Washington State where Nick was shot by Jake. She's also hoping that Jake will take a plea there.

Closing arguments are finished and the jury has left the courtroom to deliberate. The following day they have returned a verdict. Everyone scrambles to the courthouse to hear the verdict. Jake has been found guilty on all charges. His attorney requests that the court impose sentencing immediately because his client has other charges to take care of. The judge sentences Jake to death.

Jake makes plea deals with the rest of the states that have charges against him. He gets a life sentence without parole in all the other cases. Sadie is happy. She didn't want to have to testify again. The first one was bad enough. Jake gave her his stare as he did in the interrogation room. She thinks he was trying to intimidate her but it didn't work. She doesn't intimidate easily anymore.

Jake appeals his sentence. He has made friends on the inside. His appeal gets denied. He sends in a new appeal. He is allowed three appeals before he can't appeal again. He's doing the appeals to buy time. He knows that until his appeals run out they won't execute him.

It's been almost ten years later and Jake is still sitting on death row today. He filed his last appeal three years ago. Maude and Michael are still enjoying their retirement and are in their mid-seventies. Sadie and Nick are still married. Hannah is now entering college. Jonah is starting high school and their youngest, Caitlin is in middle school. Agent Malone is now retired from the FBI.